THE LEATHER DADDY AND THE FEMME

an erotic novel in several scenes
and a few conversations

Carol Queen

Down There Press
San Francisco, California

DEDICATION

This book is in tribute to Dominique Aury,
John Preston,
and Patrick Califia

and dedicated to Dr. Robert Morgan Lawrence,
my best Daddy,
without whom...

INTRODUCTION

If I had not migrated to fin de millennium San Francisco, a full-scale urban experiment in difference, who knows what shapes my sexual fantasies might have taken? They might have remained baroquely *Story of O*, even Sadean; they might have propagated alien forms with interesting new fuckable appendages. They probably would have retained the Tom of Finland edge of my nastiest, hottest reveries – an edge maintained, indeed embellished, throughout T*he Leather Daddy and the Femme* – fantasies I spun all alone and without support in my former life as a p.c. dyke. All I needed to seed them was a few glimpses of 1970s boyporn and a trip to see live, pierced daddies on Gay Day, and my imagination did the rest; they grew like Space Rocks into improbable shapes, needing no other roots in the life I lived with my girlfriends.

But without queer images, who would I have been? I have no idea. All these dreams and visions have been shaped by the people I've known and loved as well as the guilty pleasures I was never supposed to envision. As well, *The Leather Daddy and the Femme* indulges in a little queer-community philosophy, for no sex I ever had existed outside questions of who I was for having it, and even now, no sooner do I concoct a splendid jack-off scenario but I begin to wonder who these people are – and who I am for dreaming about them. Such are the ways identity politics has crept under my skin, and perhaps under yours.

This is the principal difference between the first edition of the book and this one – the first publisher didn't think talk of orientation and relationship would enhance a fuck book. I disagree, and since most people fuck within the context of relationships and sexualities, I've put that material back in.

The characters in this book are fictitious – even those who inadvertently have the same names as now-departed leathermen who lived in San Francisco in the 1970s. I did not model Jack, Randy, Demetrius, Ariel, or any of the other people who surfaced from my subconscious to populate this book, on anyone. Still, they all borrow from people I have known – certainly the San Francisco women who played with gay men during the '70s and '80s, including Cynthia Slater; and from the gay and bisexual men who were their playmates, especially my first leather daddy playmate, David Lourea, who once, amid gales of laughter, paddled me with my own high-heeled shoe while making me balance on the other one. He is missed, and not just by me. And I was forced to disappoint an avid reader who begged me to tell him that Mistress Georgia Strong was based on a real dominatrix, because if so, he wanted to book a session with her as soon as possible.

My own adventures do not appear here; my own fantasies, preferences, and desires, and my own sexual politics, do. The San Francisco I live in has a few more sources of support for queers who play across gender lines than Randy's San Francisco offers; while she frets about Jack's sexual orientation, I have friends from all across the spectrum, many of them gathered together in the Black Leather Wing of the Radical Faeries. (If you had told me when I was arguing Mary Daly with my study group back in 1979 that I would grow up to be a Radical Faerie...)

This is a sexual fantasy, meant to cross at least as many boundaries as its protagonists; and it is sited in the queer community because that is where I live, mostly, and because in the queer community experimentation and transgression happen a little more (sometimes a lot more) easily than they do outside. But the characters speak for themselves, not for the whole community, not even for any subset of the whole community they might seem at first glance to represent. I want in particular to say that my transgendered characters are not meant to represent the TS/TG community, of which I am not a member – except, wholeheartedly, in spirit. However, if these characters born within my imagination resonate with others, I am glad, even grateful. The last thing I want to do is misrepresent people who make more space and possibility for all of us.

I BEGAN WRITING and publishing the stories that became *The Leather Daddy and the Femme* in 1990. "After the Light Changed" appeared in *Taste of Latex* (the Winter '90-'91 issue), and I read it publicly at Smutfest, Lily (Burana) Braindrop's fabulous birthday party, and elsewhere. Incredibly strong reader response – more than to anything else I've to date written – told me that I was not the only woman who eroticized daddies; the characters themselves clamored for more exposure. Taking a shortcut one day down a SOMA alley I exclaimed, "Hey, that's where Jack lives!"

Other chapters appeared, in various incarnations, in *Taste of Latex*, *Black Sheets*, Laura Antoniou's *Looking for Mr. Preston* (for which I wrote "Ganged"), *Best Gay Erotica 1996*, *Best Lesbian Erotica 1997*, Pat Califia's *Doing It For Daddy*, and other anthologies. In many cases the pieces were written first to be read at clubs and other San Francisco sex/art events. The people who populate *The Leather Daddy and the Femme* emerged in stories told over several years' time; I pieced together their histories and adventures much as we gradually learn old tales from new lovers. I did so within the context of the beginning of the 1990s, the first years of what was to become a boom decade that, ironically, radically changed the San Francisco which *The Leather Daddy and the Femme* commemmorates.

Now that the book embarks on its second edition, with a

wonderful new publisher, I again have a picture of setting it like a little boat on the river that is the queer history of this city. It made enough of a mark in its first printing that I have received heartfelt complaints that it was for a while out of print, but now it can find its way back to the current and sail on.

– Carol Queen
San Francisco, April 2003

AFTER THE LIGHT CHANGED

I was looking pretty boyish that evening. Maybe that's why he looked twice at the stoplight when my car pulled up next to his motorcycle. Usually guys like that are moving, you just see a gleaming blur of black and silver. But here at the light was a real done-up daddy, sitting stock-still – except for his head, which turned in response to my eyes fixed on him and found what he saw noticeable enough to make him turn again. When boy-energy gets into me I look like an effete young Cambridge faggot looking to go bad: round spectacles framing inquisitive eyes and a shock of hair falling down over one. Not classically Daddy's Boy, something a little different. Maybe tonight this daddy was looking for a new kind of ride.

A real done-up daddy, yeah. His leathers were immaculate, carrying that dull gleam that well-kept black leather picks up under streetlights. Black leather cap, high boots, everything on him black and silver except the well-worn blue denim at his crotch, bulging invitingly out of a pair of chaps. I eyed that denimed expanse quite deliberately; he noticed. He had steely-blue daddy-eyes and a well-trimmed beard. I couldn't see his hands under the riding gloves, but they looked big, and from the looks of him I bet they were manicured. I love these impeccable daddies. They appeal to the femme in me.

And his bike! A huge shiny animal, a Harley, of course – nothing but classic for this daddy. The chrome gleamed like he did the fine polish with his tongue – or rather, used the tongue of some lucky boy. I'm more for polishing leather, myself, but if this stone-hot daddy told me to do his bike, of course I'd get right to it.

Ooh, he was looking right into my eyes, taking in my angelic Vienna-Choirboy face and my leather jacket, much rattier than his with all its ACT-UP and Queer Nation stickers. Does he think I'm cute enough for a walk on the wild side? I could hear it as he dished me to all the other daddies: "Yeah, this hot little schoolboy, looked real innocent but he cruised me like he knew what I had and wanted it, so I let him follow me home."

On the cross-street the light turned yellow. I *did* want what he had. This was it. I leaned out the window and said, just loud enough to be heard, careful to keep my voice low-pitched, "Daddy, can I come too?"

The daddy grinned. When the light turned green he gunned the Harley, took the space in front of my car, and signaled for me to follow.

An apartment South of Market – oh, this was perfect. At three a.m. on any given night he could probably open his bedroom window and find a willing mouth down here to piss in – I've *heard* about this alley. The entryway was dark. Good. I parked my car and caught up with him there. I fell to my knees as he pulled his keys from his belt. By the time he had his door unlocked I was chewing on his balls through the denim. He let me go on that way for a minute and then he collared me and hauled me into the dark foyer. I barely had time to grab my rucksack, which I'd let fall beside me so I could get both hands on his hard, leather-clad thighs.

Inside, I pulled off my glasses and tucked them away safely in my jacket. Daddy pushed me back onto my knees, and I scrambled to open the buttons of his Levi's. I wanted his cock, wanted it big, wanted it down my throat with his hands fisting the hair at the nape of my neck, giving it to me hard and rhythmic. I wanted to suck both his balls into my mouth while he slapped his dick against my cheeks. Cock worship in the dark, *Use me, Daddy, no, don't come yet – I have a surprise for you.*

I don't know how long I went on. I get lost in cocksucking sometimes, it's like a ritual, it disconnects me from my head, and when it's anonymous all the more so. I hadn't even seen this cock I was sucking, and that made me feel I could be anyone, even an adventurous gay boy in a South of Market alley, sucking Daddy's big hard dick. Any second now he could realize that I was no ordinary boy, and that gave me a great rush of adrenaline, a lust to have it down my throat. Until he discovered me I could believe this illusion myself, and with most men this was all I could expect, a cocksucker until they turned the lights on.

Daddy was moaning; guess as a cocksucker I got a passing grade. I felt the seam of my Levi's, wet where they pressed into my cunt. Jesus, I wanted it, I wanted it from him, I wanted him not to care. The scents of leather and sweat filled my head. Finally I pulled my mouth away from his dick, no problem speaking in a low voice now, shit, I was hoarse from his pounding. "Daddy, please, I want you to fuck me."

He pulled me up at once, kissed me, hard. That was a surprise. I was swooning, not feeling like a boy now, whatever a boy feels like, but all womanly, my brain in my cunt. And I was about to be discovered. His hand was sliding into my jacket; any second now it would fall upon the swell of my breast. This was where most guys freaked out and sent me home to beat off. That was okay, usually, but god, it would kill me to break this kiss.

But the kiss went on even when his fingers grazed first one breast, then the other...when his other hand followed the first under my jacket, then under my shirt, as if for corroboration, and he felt my nipples go hard under his touch. He squeezed them, eliciting a very un-boyish moan, thrusting his tongue deep down where his cock had been, so that even when he twisted my nipples into the shape of morning-glories, furled around themselves, I couldn't cry out.

The kiss went on even when one hand slid down my belly and started undoing the buttons of my jeans until there was room for him to slip a finger down between my pussy-lips, root its way, almost roughly, all the way into my cunt, pull the slick finger out again and thrust it into my mouth, where our tongues sucked it clean. The kiss lasted until he'd slid his fingers back in and fucked me all slow and juicy and excruciating and I finally broke away to beg, "Oh, Jesus, please, make me come!" He stroked in faster, then; I came like a fountain into his hand. He rubbed the juice all over my face, licked some of it off kissing me again, then pulled me down the hall into a lit room. I felt weak-kneed and wildly disheveled; he was immaculate yet, but his cock was out and it was still hard. For me.

Those steel-blue eyes were lit with more than amusement, and when he spoke, in a soft, low, almost-drawl, I realized it was the first time I'd heard his voice.

"Well, little boy, I must say you had me tricked." He laughed; I guess I looked a little proud. "Do you make a habit of fooling guys like me?"

"Not very often," I managed. "And most men don't want what they get."

"No, I would imagine not. A little too much pussy under that boy-drag. A man wouldn't want to get himself...*confused*. Hey, where'd you learn to suck cock? A bathhouse?"

"My brother taught me. He's gay."

"Shit, bring him with you the next time you visit," said the daddy. "I'll die and go to heaven." He pushed me back on the bed then and knelt above me. His big cock dangled above my face and at first he held me down, teasing me with it, but I begged and he lowered it to my lips, letting me have just enough to suck on like a baby dreams over a tit. "Good girl," he said, smiling a little, running his fingertips over my skin in a most enticing way. The boy-energy was gone, but I didn't want to stay a little girl with a man this hot. Anyway, he wasn't acting like a leather daddy any more.

I don't know what gets into me. When I cruise gay men as a boy, I know full well that I have to stay a boy the whole time. Unless they send me out at the first touch of curves, the first smell of pussy, they only want to play with me if I can keep up the fantasy. I lick Daddy's boots and suck his cock and get on my face for him, raise my ass up at the first brush of his cock on my cheeks. I beg Daddy to fuck my ass and promise I'll be his good boy, always. But deep inside, even as he's slam-fucking my ass and I'm screaming from the deep pounding pleasure of it, even though I love being a faggot for him, I secretly wish he'd slip and bury his meat all the way deep in my cunt. I love being a boy, but I don't like having to be two separate people to get what I want. I really want the men I fuck to turn me over and see the whole me: the woman in the boy, the boy in the woman. This daddy, this leatherman whose name I didn't even know, was the first one with whom that seemed possible – and I wanted to make sure. I wanted to know if he would really play with me.

So again I let his cock slip from my lips. "Daddy, will you let me up for a minute? I want to play a new game, and I really want you to like it." He released me, looking at me quizzically as I reached for my bag and pulled the last of my clothes off. There. A femme hates having pants bagging around her ankles.

Feeling sleeker already, I took the bag into the bathroom, promising I'd be right back. Everything there – shoes, clothes, makeup. It was time to grow up.

The dress was red and tight and hugged my small breasts

into cleavage. Its backline plunged down almost to the swell of my ass. Black stockings and garters (the dress was too tight to wear a belt under, only a black g-string), and red leather pumps with high, high heels. The kind of shoes drag queens named so aptly "Come-Fuck-Me-Pumps." You're not supposed to walk in them, you're supposed to offer the toe to a worshipful tongue, or lock them around a neck while you get pounded. Which is what I hoped would be happening to me shortly.

With some gel and a brush my hair went from boyish to chic. Powder on my face, then blush. I darkened my eyebrows and lashes, lined and shaded my eyes with green and violet, and brushed deep crimson onto my lips. An amazingly changed face, all angles and shadows and eyes and cheekbones, looked back at me from the mirror. One last glance: I was sufficiently stunning. In fact, the sight, combined with the knowledge that I was about to emerge from the little room into the leather daddy's view, had me soaked, my heart pounding, my clit buzzing. I get so very narcissistic when I'm femmed out. I want to reach for my image in the mirror, take her apart and fuck her. No doubt I'd be riding this energy into the girl-bars tomorrow night, looking for my image stepped through the looking glass, out looking for me.

One last flourish, a long sheer black scarf, sheer as my stockings, flung around my shoulders, hiding nothing. I stepped back into the leather daddy's room.

He'd taken his jeans off from beneath the chaps. His jacket was off, too, hung carefully over a chair. His dick was in his hand. He'd been stroking it, staying hard. Bands of leather drew my gaze to the hard curves of his biceps. Silver rings gleamed in his nipples. I felt like a *Vogue* model who'd stumbled into a Tom of Finland painting. He was gorgeous. He was every bit the spectacle I was, body modified and presented to evoke heat, to attract sex.

He looked at me hard, taking in the transformation. I saw his cock jump; good.

"So, Daddy, do you still want to play?" I said "Daddy" in a different voice this time, let it be lush with irony, like a '40s burlesque queen. A well-educated faggot ought to pick up on that.

There was a touch of wonder in his voice. "God damn. I don't believe I've ever picked up anything quite like you." Then suspicion. "So what's your trip? Trying to turn the heathens into hets? No wonder all those other guys threw you out."

A new rush of adrenaline hit. *Go ahead*, I thought, *be uncomfortable, baby, but don't stop wanting it*. I took a couple of steps, coming near enough the bed that I could put one foot up on it. I moved into his territory, gave him a view of the tops of my stockings and the wet, pussy-redolent g-string. I narrowed my eyes. "Did I suck your cock like a het? You think I can't take it now that I have a dress on?"

He persisted. "Why waste this on gay men? Straight boys must fall over for you."

"Straight boys don't know how to give me what I want." I ran my eyes down his body. "Besides, your cock says I'm not wasting this on you."

He made no move to try to hide the hard-on. His voice was more curious than accusatory when he said, "You get a perverse charge out of this, don't you?"

"Yeah, I do. But I really want *you* to get a perverse charge out of it." I moved to him, knelt over him so that only the insides of my knees touched the smooth leather of the chaps. He was close enough to touch; I had to stop from reaching. This was it, the last obstacle. His hard cock almost touched me. "I'm no ordinary boy, Daddy, and I'm no ordinary woman. Do you want it? Just take it."

There is so much power in being open and accessible and

ready. So much power in wanting it. That's what so many other women don't understand. You'll never get what you want if you make it too hard for someone to give it to you. He proved it: He lifted his hands to me, ran them once over my body, bringing the nipples up hard through the clinging dress, pinned my arms at my sides and brought me down into a kiss that seared and melted, a kiss I felt like a tongue in my cunt. I felt myself sliding along his body until his cockhead rested against the soaked silk of my g-string, hard and hot, and he stroked against my clit over and over and over. When he released my arms, one big hand held my ass, keeping me pushed against him. The other hand was fisted in my hair. He held me fast, and once again my cries of orgasm were muffled on his tongue.

When his mouth left mine it went to my ear, talking low.

"Pretty girl, I want your cunt so hot you go crazy. You got all dressed up for me, didn't you? Pretty bitch, you want it rough, you like it like that?"

"Yes!" I gasped, still riding the last waves of come, wanting more.

"Then tell me. Ask for it. Beg me!"

He pulled the scarf from around my neck, threw me easily onto my back. He pinned my arms over my head, bound my wrists with the scarf, talking in his low daddy-voice, playing my game:

"You want it, pretty bitch? You're going to get it, Miss Special. So you think your cunt is good enough for my meat? Can't get what you need from straight boys? You're gonna need it bad before you get an inch of me, baby...spread 'em, that's right, spread for me, show it to me, let me have a good look. I haven't seen one of these in a real long time...you know what I usually do with this cock, don't you? Is that what you want, is that what straight boys don't give you? Want it in your ass, make you be Daddy's boy again, hmmmm? No, you want it in your pussy, baby, I can feel it. Just shove it all inside you, you want to feel it open you up, can you take it?" He rolled me over.

Now he was reddening my ass with slaps, the dress pulled up to my waist, and from nowhere he clicked open a knife. I gasped and whimpered, but he just used it to cut the g-string off and it disappeared again. He slapped my pussy with his cock, scattering drops of my wetness, stopping short before I came, whispering, "Want it, pretty bitch? Want it all?" And I writhed against him and begged him:

"Jesus, please, give it to me, Daddy! Please...*please!*"

He was a consummate tease, this daddy; I wondered dimly if his boys tried to wiggle their assholes onto his just-out-of-reach cock the way I was trying to capture it with my hungry cunt. Not so much difference between one hunger and another, after all.

He reached for a rubber, worked it over his cockhead and rolled it down the shaft. The encasement made his big cock strain harder. As he knelt between my spread-wide legs, I murmured, "Give it to me, give it to me, give..." – and in a long plunge, he did.

It felt so good to be filled so full, with the smell of hot leather and cock and pussy and the feel of the chaps against my legs. The second thrust came harder than the first, and a look of sexy concentration played across my leather daddy's face as he settled in for a long, hard, pounding ride.

It was my turn to talk to him as I met his strokes with thrusts of my own, letting my pinned-down body fill with delicious tension that would build up to even more intense peaks.

"Oh, yeah, just like that, give me your cock, baby, fill up my pussy, yeah...give it to me, give it to me, you know I can take it, hard, yeah, come on...fuck my cunt like you fuck your boys' asses, make me take it from you, yeah, don't stop, don't ever stop, just try to outlast me, Daddy – you can fuck me all

night, fill that rubber with a big hot load and I'll come just thinking about you, just give it to me...just give it to me, make me,
make me...come..."

And it was all lost in cries and sobs and breath taking over.
Somehow he'd untied my hands and I held him and came and
came and came, and the wild ride was over with half a dozen
bucking thrusts. I heard his yells mingle with mine, and I
reached down to pull cock and rubber free of my cunt and feel
the heft of jism in my hand as we lay together in a tangle of
sweaty limbs, not man and woman, just animals, two sated animals.

I drifted off to sleep and woke again as he was working the
tight, sweaty dress over my head and off. My red leather shoes
glowed against the white sheets.

"Hellion," he said as my eyes opened, "faggot in a woman's
body, bitch-goddess, do you intend to sleep in your exquisite
red shoes?"

I held them up for him to take off, one and then the other,
and he placed respectful kisses on each toe before he set them
on the bed.

"No," I said, "that's too femmy, even for me."

"And what does a man need to do with you around," he
continued, pulling off my stockings, "to get fucked? Call your
brother?"

He hadn't seen all the contents of my trick bag. I reached for
it and spilled it onto the floor: three dildos, a harness and a pair
of long rubber gloves fell out. I promised that in the morning he
could take his pick. I was dying to show Daddy what else a
femme can do.

THE NEXT MORNING

I woke to the sound of shower spray hitting tile, and for a minute I stayed groggy, listening to the hum of water in the pipes, not entirely sure where I was. I was drifting in and out of a dream, something about Harleys and red leather shoes. I heard a motorcycle rev and catch outside, and it twined itself into my dream, not waking me. But when the bike gunned and roared away, it shocked me into alertness and I remembered where I was, recognized the leather daddy's spare, neat room, and his face swam into my consciousness: I saw him pulling my pumps off and kissing each toe.

He wasn't next to me, though the bed was tousled as if two people had fucked here and then shared it in sleep. For a minute I was afraid the bike I'd heard outside was his, that he'd gone off and left me to wake in his bed and let myself out of his alley apartment. Well, maybe he'd only gone out to get us coffee and croissants or something. I wasn't sure he looked like the kind of guy who made his own coffee.

But no, I heard water running in the next room. He must be in the shower. Thinking about him naked and wet in a steamy room started giving me ideas. I hoped he had lots of hot water.

Stretching like a just-roused cat, I rolled out of bed. My red dress and red shoes were neatly laid over the arm of the room's one chair. The other arm, like a tireless valet, held his chaps. I remembered he had taken them, with his wrist and bicep cuffs, off before he returned to bed and allowed me to curl up under his musky-scented armpit. The cuffs lay with his worn leather riding gloves on the dresser-top. I picked the gloves up and drew in a long breath of the leather, redolent of his man-smell and the machine-smell of the bike, and placed them carefully back where he'd put them when he took them off.

Over the dresser hung an old silver-backed mirror with a simple, polished wooden frame, the kind of mirror his granddad had probably had. With my fingers I combed my hair into some semblance of presentability, and I rubbed away the mascara that overnight had migrated into a raccoon mask around my eyes. That was really the most embarrassing part of being a femme, I reflected; the desire to be fucked into a stupor was definitely incompatible with wearing makeup, at least when the fucking happened right before bed.

I was not concerned with resurrecting my femme look now, however. The leather daddy already knew who I was, in that respect at least. In the whole room the only thing out of place, besides the rumpled bedclothes, was my upended trick bag. I picked up my harness and strapped it on, then chose a dildo from the three in my bag, a big one. If everything continued to go as well as it had last night, the daddy would get his morning fuck. In the full-length mirror on the closet door I surveyed myself. Very much a woman, and a big latex dick curving up where you'd expect a clit to be. I rolled a condom onto the dick and opened the bathroom door.

He was there, all right; I saw his silhouette through the opaque glass of the shower door. The glass diffused the image of the moving man inside. I watched him for a minute before I moved any closer, tightening the straps of the harness, a nylon one unlike the leather I usually wore. I'd just bought it on a lark, thinking maybe I'd want to fuck somebody in a hot tub some-day and would need something waterproof – now the day was here. Reflexively I stroked the dildo, my cock now, feeling its heft. It pressed tight against my clit, and stroking it sent little waves of pleasure through me.

I jacked off for a few minutes, wondering if he'd jack off to *my* silhouette in a shower. Then I decided it was time to step inside. I had butterflies; I always do before fucking somebody new. This was different from spreading my legs to someone's hand or cock, this was scarier. Strapping on a cock means strapping on a new kind of responsibility. I'm glad I don't have it all the time.

He was aware of my presence the minute my hand touched the door, and it was like he'd been waiting for me, waiting to see if I'd take the initiative by coming in to find him. His skin shone in the water and the rivulets that streamed down his body looked like sweat on a hot, hot day; his wet hair shone too, sleek as a seal's. Seeing him naked I caught my breath; seeing my cock, he caught his.

He pulled me to him to kiss me and I felt the beat of the water and his mouth at the same time as the shower rained down warm on us. His hand went right to my cock, and every stroke pressed the dildo into my clit. It made my cunt as hot and wet as all the rest of me.

The big shower, twice the size of an ordinary one, was tiled with small grey flag, dark as wet pavement under the shower spray. It had a tiled bench. It also had a fancy showerhead, and he reached up and switched the spray to a fine mist, fine enough to breathe through, like a San Francisco fog but hot. Then he knelt to me and took the head of my cock in his lips.

He sucked it like it was real. I could feel each tug of his mouth on my clit. And I could have sworn I remembered how it felt, from another life nearly forgotten, exactly how it felt to have a dick that could feel lips and teeth and tongue. I felt a resurgence of the amazement, the miracle I'd felt the night before: I'd found a man who would really *play* with me.

The daddy had my asscheeks in his hands, kneeling to me, throating my dick. The latex gave me a dim reflection of the sensations a flesh and blood cock would: I felt the cockhead pop in and out of the ring of muscle at his throat. No gag reflex at all – Jesus, this man was impressive. He growled around the dick, bit it, used my ass to pull me down his throat. I rested my hands on his hard shoulders, letting him control the pace, and felt orgasm simmering from the rhythm of the dildo on my clit and the pressure of his big hands squeezing and parting my cheeks. He sucked just a little too slowly to make me come – maybe on purpose. I got lost in the building sensation just as I had the night before when it had been his cock in my throat.

Gradually he picked up the pace. I laced my hands around the back of his head, just to make sure he wasn't going to stop on me, but he showed no signs of flagging. Pushing me back so the the warm wet tile supported me, he tumbled me into a blinding orgasm, and my first awareness when I came to was his voice in my ear, low: "Yeah, come for me, shoot it, baby, I want that load, I want it all...."

"My cock's still hard, Daddy," I said, and ran my hands down his belly and grasped his dick, harder still. "It's hard for you – are you gonna get back on your knees for me? Are you gonna let me slide my big cock deep into you?"

That got his attention. He made a sound that fell somewhere between his cocksucking growl and a whimper, and he reached past me and came up with a tube of K-Y.

"Lube it, baby. Lube my cock, that's right, get it slick. I'm gonna slide my cock up your ass. I'm gonna fuck you, Daddy."

My cunt humming, I felt the foreshadow of another orgasm just from talking to him that way, just from reading the hungry energy of his response. I had the feeling I'd finally found someone with as complicated a sexuality as mine, for it was clear that he wanted it as badly from me now as I'd wanted it from him the night before.

He didn't lube it right away. He went for my dick with his mouth again, sucking so hard on it that I came again just from the insistent, rhythmic throb of the dildo's base on my clit. I yelled this time, and the sound reverberated, mixed with the hissing sound the water made on the wall of the shower stall. My dick was shiny with the thick saliva from his throat. It glittered on the black rubber.

I liked how surreal it looked, shiny black like that, but suddenly wished I'd brought the realistic-looking dick. Would that make it hotter for him, seeing veins and skin-like latex, Jeff Stryker's movable balls to squeeze? For a man in love with cock, how could this stylized one do the trick?

But he was growling in his throat again and I saw him stroking his own meat, the veins on it pulsing a little with each new hot gush of blood they let in, and I relaxed, remembered the time an old lover had undone her 501s to reveal a dildo tucked in and covered by her shirttail. I'd been in the bar with her for an hour and hadn't even noticed, until she came into the restroom stall with me, stood before me as I peed, and loosed each button. When the dick popped out she ever so delicately took my chin in her hand and brought my lips to the head of the thing. It was lavender silicone and not shaped like a cock at all. It wasn't even *meant* to be a cock, on her. She never got especially turned on to cocks – but strapping on something to fuck with, something that let her pin me to a bed or a wall and let her cunt-energy come exploding out of her and into *my* cunt or asshole, she liked *that* just fine. Still pissing, I took her dildo between my teeth, sucked it in deep so the slime from my throat would make it slick enough to shove into me hard when she raised me, turned my face to the wall, my skirt up around my waist, her fingers finding my clit and rubbing it with the last drops of my piss.

She didn't think of it as a cock so I didn't either, but I sure did take it seriously...so maybe the daddy, reaching for the lube now, *really* wanted this cock, my cock, even if I wasn't hung like Jeff Stryker.

So I told him to get on his knees; I told him to give me his ass. He anointed my cock and it glistened in the hot fog of the shower. He took a high crouch, bracing himself with his hands on the low bench. He growled one more time, rubbed his ass up and down my thighs, trying to capture the dildo just like I'd tried to grab his cock with my pussy the night before. The growl turned to words: he was saying "C'mon. Put it in. *Fuck* me." My sleek daddy had metamorphosed into a horny weasel with a voracious asshole – and I knew just how he felt. I didn't have the heart to tease him, and besides, I was horny myself for the feeling of his asshole smoothly beginning to open for my dick.

I angled my cock towards his ass. The next sweep he made against me slid his hole right up against my cockhead, just where I wanted him. He stopped moving, with a shudder and a moan, and leaned back against the lubed rubber dick. The pressure began to open his asshole – no surprise, he was easy.

I pulled back just a little. He actually whimpered, thought I was teasing him, but I grabbed his hips to pull him against me, pumping him fast but not hard enough for the tip of the dildo to pop all the way in. A couple of minutes of that will drive any fuck-starved man or woman insane; *I* ought to know. He still tried to thrust back onto my cock, but I held his hips harder, told him with my body that even as I had given him control to fuck me last night, I would take it now, take it when and how I wanted him. A fuck is almost always better for that kind of energy; I just wanted him off-balance enough to really need it.

That was a gamble – until now I'd only known him as a top-man, and a consummate one at that. I was already hoping he played rougher games and that I'd have the chance to give myself over to his will again. The only indication I'd had that he might be willing to bottom at all – much less to a strange, gender-schitzed boygirl from out of nowhere – was the sight of him kissing the toes of my shoes as he undressed me and laid me down to share his bed.

But the daddy had responded so immediately when I signaled my willingness to play, took me so smoothly, met me so completely, that I had a feeling he'd like being flipped – it would be just as hot to be taken as to take. I'd never tried this

24

with a man, much less a gay one. But I'd met a couple of butch women whose savoir-faire was really an open invitation to lay them down and fist them. Besides, I was trusting my intuition, and right now my intuition was operating out of the head of my dick. My intuition was about to sink balls-deep into his ass.

In one fast motion, on the backthrust, I released my hold on his hips. By the time I was thrusting forward I had thrown my arms around his chest and gotten him by the tits. I pulled him against me and my dick sank home.

That one long stroke, the one he'd been waiting for, made him come – I felt his asshole pulse around my cock, buried deep in him now, and he moaned and gasped as I slowly, slowly started to fuck him, hardly pulling out at all, a slow deep fuck while I worked his nipples and began to whisper how good he was, how good he could take it, how good I was gonna give it to him, how fine he was with my big cock in his butt, taking it from me so nice and slow.

Then I got my footing and pulled almost all the way out. He swallowed hard, braced.

"That's right, baby," I said, almost a croon, "you know what comes next, don't you? What am I gonna do with my cock, Daddy? What am I going to do to you?"

"Fuck me," he said in his cocksucking voice, "you're gonna fuck me." His ass was in the air. My black rubber dick shone in the water-diffused light. He was the most gorgeous fucking thing I'd ever seen, a strong nasty man impaled on my cock. If only I could give it to him right. If only I could fuck him as perfectly as he had fucked me. Before I went any further I ran my hands down his belly, over his cock. Still straining hard – he hadn't shot yet, only orgasmed with pulses of his cock and asshole and pelvic muscles – just like me, he could come without shooting. He didn't know it yet, but I could also come and shoot, just like him, spray my lighter jizz in a scented gush.

My touch made him shudder. I had the sudden thought, accompanied by a hot pulse in my cunt, that he would take anything from me now. Fuck sex differences, fuck "men are..." and "women are..." He was giving himself to me just as I had given myself to him. Penetrated, in submission, ass poised and open to me: He was mine.

I took him, not slow, not soft. I knew what he wanted. I wanted to give it to him so bad I could taste the adrenaline. I slammed my cock into his ass. I spread his cheeks with my hands, watched, mesmerizing myself, as my hips took hold of a rhythm so primal it seemed my brain had nothing at all to do with it. I pumped him as hard as I could, pumped him until we were both growling. I chanted "Take it! *Take* it!" – and he interrupted his alleycat-getting-fucked noise only with an occasional guttural "Yeah! *Fuck!*"

I had him by the throat. One of my feet was braced on the bench. He thrust his body back as hard and fast as I was thrusting in. I knew I wasn't strong enough to strangle him, but I had him just right: I could throttle him into dizziness, almost to passing out, into a vast, almost-orgasmic plane where it would feel like getting buttfucked on a cloud in heaven. I could keep him there or bring him back just by varying the pressure. The powerful feeling of having him in my hands was filling my heart as well as my cunt.

Suddenly I was acutely aware that I did not know his name. We were so raw with each other, so right, too – so *intimate* – even if he *did* sex like this with all his tricks. But nameless. That was hot and frightening in equal measure. It gave me both more power and less.

I changed my stroke. I angled my cock so it pumped over his prostate, and under my hands and through my dick I felt him soar up toward orgasm. I moved my hands from his throat back to his rampant cock, and my touch triggered him. With a guttural cry he shot five long, wrenching pulses into my hands, and I sank into him deeply, teeth holding the back of his neck like a cat does when it's fucking. His asshole clenched on my cock, his skin and muscle between my teeth, I thought about bringing my hand full of his jism to my lips, thought of licking the cream off my fingers – *can't* – and so I brought the hand to his mouth instead, thrust four fingers in for him to suck his own juice off me. The hot suction of mouth on fingers triggered me into a come so strong I thought I was going to cry. I held him tightly from behind and we collapsed onto the shower floor.

I BECAME AWARE again, slowly, of the hot mist. We lay all tangled the way we had the night before, a long time, silent except for our breath as it slowly returned to normal. At last he moved his hand away from where it had been resting on my thigh and pulled my dildo free of his ass. I loosed the harness's buckles with one hand and slipped it off, my pussy returning to nestle tightly against his butt, my hand reaching around to rest on his softening cock. The silence felt neither uncomfortable nor natural, for now we both looked for a way past the fact that we did not know each other. I was tempted to pull his hand to my cunt, start us sexing again, just so we wouldn't have to talk, just to avoid breaking the spell. He closed his big hand around my hand, the one that held his dick. With the pressure I became aware of my pulse, beating fast. His thumb and forefinger closed around my wrist – he was feeling it too. That or he was measuring to see how well it would fit in his ass.

My mind raced in the silence. I was developing a case of nerves, which seemed stupid, since five minutes before I'd been playing "Realm of the Senses" with a man who I now couldn't think of a way to talk to. Opening lines spun through my head, but I felt too nervous to use them.

He shifted onto his back and pulled me on top of him. Seeing his big-dicked alley-cat girl in a lather of shyness he laughed and wrapped his arms around me and, mercifully, let me off the hook.

"We should probably have gotten introductions out of the way last night, little hellion," he said. "I didn't quite bargain on having this kind of a morning. I didn't bargain on ever meeting up with anything like you, in fact. I'm not even sure you're real, except my asshole's still pulsing. Do you have a name?"

"I have two names," I said. "The one you picked up last night is Randy. The one you fucked is Miranda."

"Which one is with me now?"

I shook my head. "Not sure. I'm off-center right now. Maybe I'm in transition from one to the other. You're not supposed to be real either, you know."

"If you're doubting my existence after fucking me into the middle of next week I guess I'd really better introduce myself. I'm Jack Prosper, and I assure you I am real, but you can keep calling me Daddy for as long as you want, dear, and I must say I *never* wind up on the floor of the shower with my tricks. Did your brother teach you to fuck ass, too?"

I giggled and nodded. "But I've had a little practice elsewhere. Girls like to get butt-fucked too, you know. *Some* girls."

Jack shook his head. "Until last night, I hadn't given any thought to what girls like – not for a lot of years. But I don't think you bear much resemblance to the girls I used to know. You're queer as a three-dollar bill, for one thing. Are there more out there like you?"

I frowned a little. "Some. Not very many."

"Must be frustrating to be the weirdest gal on the block."

"Jack...Daddy...I don't want to talk about this right now." I'd turned almost petulant, buried my nose in his armpit to try to keep from thinking how unlikely it was that Jack and I would be able to relate in broad daylight, with our clothes on. Boys and girls, what a mess. Girls and girls were almost as bad. It was true that I had a hard time finding lovers willing to follow me all over the gender-and-sex landscape. If I wasn't too queer I was too kinky. If I wasn't too kinky I was too insatiable. If I wasn't that I was too slutty or even too serious. All of a sudden I was worried that Jack would realize who he'd stuck his butt in the air for, have an episode of heterosexual panic, and throw me out.

He was kind of psychic, though. "You're too much for most

people, aren't you, Randy-Miranda? Just too queer. What do you think, I'm gonna decide I don't want my dick to smell like fish?" I glared at him, then frowned and nodded. "Child, any faggot who'd kick a love goddess with a big dick out of bed is insane, I don't care what anybody says. I don't give a fuck that you're a girl. Last I checked, you creatures were receiving far different socialization. I'll just consider this a little science project."

I burst out laughing at that, couldn't help it.

"Besides, I believe you implied earlier that you could fist me. I've never been fisted by a woman before, and none of my friends have either. I don't think. And I *will* try anything once. You're such a complicated little animal, I might have to try you more than once. In the interests of science, you understand. Miss Miranda, how about another date?"

He rolled me onto my back and kissed me, just like the first kiss last night that undid me.

I'm a leather daddy's science project, I thought fuzzily as my hands found his nipple rings and tugged on them. I would crawl on my belly like a human reptile straight through the flames of hell for kisses like this. He sucked on my lower lip and my cunt started to involuntarily spasm. When we came up for breath, only for a second, I whispered, "I don't think *this* date is over yet, Daddy" – and pulled him back down.

AT THE BLACK ROSE

I shared an apartment on the upper slopes of the Tenderloin with Ariel, who used to be my lover but had since transmogrified, in true queer San Francisco fashion, into my best friend and roommate. Before Jack, she was the person with whom I'd had the most splendid and outrageous adventures. In fact, Ariel was a splendid, outrageous adventure with every breath she took.

I went home and told her about my night.

"Look what the cat dragged in! You do know it's been twenty-four hours since you went out? I had to restrain myself from calling the police." Ariel was teasing – probably. "But then I figured the cops would be afraid to go anywhere you were likely to be, so I forgot about it."

"Ariel, I met this guy! A real honest-to-god leather daddy! Let's go out for Thai food so I can tell you."

"Miranda, you weren't frequenting some Society of Janus slave auction, I hope?"

"No, Ariel! He's a real fag! He sucked my cock and every-thing! That waterproof harness works great, by the way. Come on, get your coat."

She dug a big fuzzy faux fur swing coat out of the closet. "I love this city. You found a leather daddy to fuck. I just made a hundred bucks letting a guy walk around wearing my high heels. This town is a real Mixmaster."

THE FIRST TIME I visited the Black Rose, the Tenderloin bar

where things are rarely what they seem, I was with Dave, a bisexual man with a taste for having it all wrapped up in one neat package. At the Rose he could find a beautiful woman, make an arrangement, and when he raised her glittery skirt, find a succulent cock to suck. The tits wouldn't be fake, either, at least no more fake than you find on most porn stars these days, and Dave was happier with the divine androgynes he met at the Rose than he was with anyone else in his life.

"Of course it's hard to find a girlfriend there," he said, "unless you have a lot of money, 'cause most of them are working to save up for their change. I always found it very hard to be lovers with a working girl. I have too much ego."

The first time I went to the Rose, on Dave's arm, the bar was full of larger-than-life women who looked at me suspiciously, and only the ones who knew Dave came up to speak to us. The men in the bar didn't give me a second look. It wasn't that the queens didn't look like women – most of them did – but that I didn't look enough like *them*. If there was one thing the men at the Rose weren't looking for, it was a woman in jeans with no makeup.

Dave told me sometimes straight couples cruised the Rose together, but not often, so most of the girls who worked out of the bar ignored any potential I might have had to be a real pay-for-play client. I was only looking that night, anyway, and I wasn't sure it was okay for me to do even that. The Black Rose was a mirror world, a deep secret, and the only safe space most of its habitués had. It wasn't set up to welcome tourists, unless they had money to spend.

The second time I visited the Rose, I went alone.

I DIDN'T GO THERE to cruise or to trick, exactly. I think I cabbed in to the Tenderloin because I knew I could get lost there, because in a weird way the Rose was a safe space for me too, a place where I was almost invisible. When the doorman looked askance at me I mentioned Dave's name; that got me in without further hassle. I took a tiny table off to the side, where I could nurse a drink and see the stage. Sometime after ten o'clock the shiny strips of silver Mylar that curtained the back of the stage began to rustle, and seconds later the first of a dozen transsexuals came through to do her act, lip-syncing and dancing to thirty years' worth of diva tunes. As I swallowed stinging mouthfuls of a bad martini I wondered if something about Judy Garland, Tina Turner, Madonna, Aretha Franklin and Annie Lennox actually lured boys away from being boys.

It resembled a gay drag show, but not entirely – less campy by far, although some of the performers were certainly so bad they were good. Huge happy girls towered in their high shoes, barely managing to walk. The Thais, Vietnamese and Filipinas – some of the Latinas too – passed flawlessly, smooth-skinned and no taller than me. Dave had told me that the biggest secret was to get on hormones before the end of puberty. Hardly any of them could do this. Some bore scars from inexpert electrolysis.

She approached my miniature table with none of the attitude I'd gotten from the others. She stood over six feet tall in her heels – the girls at the Rose never, ever wore flats – and she was gorgeous in the bigger-than-life way I was still getting used to. Looking up at her I saw legs for miles, crazy with patterned black lace stockings, a short, shiny silver skirt topping them, and a loose, silky black tank top which didn't quite expose her breasts but showed cleavage. A tattoo peeked out – a rose, probably red but appearing black in the bar's low light. She walked easily in her high heels, had the milky baby breasts that hormones grow. The drink she brought with her was blue and shimmery. Leave it to a girl like this to drink Blue Moons. She put it down right next to my martini.

"May I join you?" she said. Her smoky voice would, if heard over the phone, have given no clue as to her gender.

"Please," I replied, and scrambled to pull a chair from the next table over for her. She took a second to settle in. Close up I could see the brown roots showing in her cascade of honey-blonde hair, could see her light lipstick carefully drawn on and the eyebrows plucked and shaped. Her skin was smoother than some of the others' and her hands were long. Her nails were clipped short – she was the only one I'd seen without long nails, I realized – but polished ruby red.

"I've never seen you here before," she said. "At first I thought you might be here to watch one of your friends perform, but you don't seem to know anybody. Is this your first time?"

"My second," I said, and told her about Dave. She knew him, of course, and dropping his name had the same effect it had had with the doorman. It meant I was safe, in on the secret. Dave was one of the few guys a lot of the girls would date without exchanging money. I asked my new friend if she'd been out with him, mostly to make conversation. With a small smile, she shook her head.

"I don't date men," she said. "I work them."

That's how I met Ariel.

BEFORE LONG I WONDERED if she was working me too. She was seductive, touching me while we talked, looking right into my eyes while I answered her questions. I had a hundred dollar bill in my pocket and I began to think about giving it to her. What fraction of the money she needed would one hundred dollars be? What would she want to do with me in return? I had some things I was trying to stop myself from thinking about the night I went to the Rose, and Ariel began to seem like a perfect way to forget them, better by far than ordering another martini or even sitting through the rest of the stage show.

"What are you thinking about, Miranda?"

"My intentions are becoming indecent. You're weaving quite a spell, Ariel."

"Oh, good." Ariel's hand, under the table, ranged up my thigh.

"The thing that has me confused is, are you working tonight? I mean, I know this is a working bar."

"I told you, I work *men*," said Ariel. She gestured around

the bar, and indeed there were a lot of men there, all driven by their fascination by the queens. Some were dressed as workmen and some had on expensive suits; I remembered, as if I'd forgotten it, that I was the only one in the Rose who didn't have or had never had a cock. Once I'd have thought of it as a place for closeted gay men. Now I knew it was more complicated than that. How I fit in as a genetic woman, though, wasn't at all clear to me.

But it was to Ariel. "I don't take money from women," she said. "I already made enough today. If you're feeling like a high-roller, you can buy me breakfast."

ARIEL'S APARTMENT was close by, one of those beautiful old Tenderloin flats that you'd never expect to find in a rundown building on a mean street. The walk home with her screwed up all my butch/femme cues. Usually I'm femme-of-center, if not aspiring to divahood, myself – at least, when I'm not a boy. But Ariel brought out none of my boyish side. Out of my desire to melt into the woodwork at The Black Rose, I'd butched it up a little – jeans and a leather jacket, flat shoes. Ariel was much more femme than me, yet she took up so much space. She strode up Jones Street like it belonged to her, and I felt small by her side, like I needed her protection. She held the door for me, and then I held the elevator for her. This walk wasn't giving me any clues about who might do what to whom.

Inside she bolted the door, kicked off her heels, and pushed me up against the hallway wall. She kissed me hard while she pulled my jacket off, leaving it in a heap on the floor. Her long hands unbuckled my belt and tugged up my shirt, mouth never leaving mine, and I touched her through the slippery, glossy fabric of the clothes she wore. When I got to her breasts I felt the firm enclosure of a push-up bra trapping them into cleavage – she moaned when I found the clasp and freed them, rubbing away the marks of the underwires, raising her nipples up with strokes of my palms. And still we kissed.

Up til then it had been an experiment, but her kiss bought and sold me. I wondered how often she found women who wanted her, how long it had been since she'd brought someone home for play, not work, how many she had to convince and what she had to do to overcome the voices in their heads clamoring, "But she's not really a..."

That's not exactly what my inner voices had been clamoring. Like I said, I had some things I was looking to forget. And five minutes into what felt like the sweetest, hungriest kiss I'd ever been lost in, still leaning together against the inside of her apartment door, I'd forgotten everything except this tall, sexy tornado who was sweeping me away from everything, whose small new breasts just filled my hands, who had my nipples between her fingers, pulling, while she devoured my mouth and my cunt got wetter and wetter.

Her bed had red sheets. It glowed like a ruby in her pale room, and finally she led me there, pulled the rest of my clothes from me, and told me to put my hands over my head and hold onto the bars of the headboard. "I won't need to tie you up," she purred, "if you're a good girl and stay right there." For an instant I wanted to disobey her – to feel her bind me, capture me, maybe get rough – but in the end I did what she said, wanting to please her, wanting to show her I was there, hot for her, there because I wanted to be.

Now I knew why Ariel groomed herself differently from the long-nailed queens at the Rose. She spread my legs wide, pulled on a latex glove, reached across me to the nightstand for lube, and then began working fingers into my ass. "Don't move your hands," she whispered, while hers invaded me, one long finger at a time, first working in and then starting to fuck – repeating again and again until she had three up my ass and I was as stretched out and full as I'd ever been. Her other hand, ruby ring glinting in the low light from a streetlamp, lay splayed across my belly, holding me down, thumb slowly working my clit, while she fucked my ass with the other. I held the bars but soon writhed crazily with the sensation, and as she fucked me more and more fiercely I raised my legs to her shoulders, spreading my ass as wide to her as I could, wanting to let her get at me as deeply as possible. When she felt my body tighten up in an imminent come, she stopped playing with my clit altogether, pulled my nipple hard, and I orgasmed from her pumping hand alone, coming until I was curled up practically sobbing – but still holding the bars.

"You're so good!" I gasped when she was finally done with me, and she gave me that small smile again and said, "What I like about assholes is, everybody has one."

I STILL DIDN'T KNOW if she had a cock. After she had my ass I lay panting and swimming in the afterglow of all the sensation, til finally I had recovered sufficiently to explore her. Her skin was soft, her body an intriguing combination of curves and muscles, almost but not quite womanly.

I pulled her skirt off, ran my hands all over the firm swell of her ass, which she raised so I could get her panties off. Underneath I found still more fabric, a dense shiny lycra clinging tightly to the curve of her crotch. Rubbing my hand across it, like I would any pussy, Ariel writhed from the pleasure, then whispered, "Go ahead, take it off too."

The lycra peeled away and revealed it, still soft, the hair compressed around it from the tight gaff she wore to hide its bulge. Was this the moment men paid her for, to see the unimaginable – a cock on a woman? Was she ashamed of it?

"Nice clit, girl," I breathed, petting it top to bottom so it stayed, for the moment, in its tucked and flattened position. "Big." Ariel's laugh didn't have any shame in it, and before long her big clit was in my mouth, getting only a little hard as I flicked my tongue across it. "Can you come this way?" I raised my head long enough to ask, and she nodded, gasped, "But I hardly ever ejaculate any more." I slid a couple of fingers up her ass while I worked her clit, and I knew when she came because her hips rose up off the bed and her hands clutched at the red sheets.

She came again, and so did I, over and over, when she rolled me onto the bottom and thrust against me like a classic tribade, her sex and mine rubbing ecstatically together. She got a little harder doing this, but not much, and it felt perfect, her ass in my hands, rocking and humping, while we kissed or sucked up red roses of blood nearly to the surface of each others' necks.

SHE BROUGHT ME COFFEE in the morning. There she was in the light of day, makeup off, naked, still easily six feet tall, rangy and baby-titted like an adolescent. Gorgeous in a way I'd never seen anyone be gorgeous before. After only one night with her I was starting to see the world and its possibilities in a new way.

"Ariel," I began, "I've got a million questions to ask you...."

"Don't they all," she said, but she kissed me.

I started to ask them over breakfast.

GANGED

Jack and I had been running together for several weeks. He knew which bar I hung out in; a couple of times he had sauntered in and found me there. He didn't stay to meet my friends; he'd haul me out and back to his South of Market apartment. We usually only got as far as the alley before his dick was out.

He had been to my apartment only once. It was more comfortable at his place; he didn't have any housemates, whereas I could never predict when Ariel would come home, half the time dragging a john. Not that Ariel would have minded the interruption, but her tricks always seemed scared of being seen. Men paying for sex acted like they were always expecting to be recognized and exposed. When I said this to Ariel she just shrugged. "In some towns they publish the names of busted johns. They have a certain right to their paranoia. I just try not to encourage it."

So mostly my relationship with Jack developed within the charmed and secret space of his rooms.

The one time he was at my place, though, I found him nosing around my room when I came in from the kitchen where I'd gone to get us something to drink. At the bedside table he picked up a book – a very battered copy of *Mr. Benson*. He grinned, and slung himself on my bed as though he habitually lounged there to read. He held the book in his left hand and of course it fell right open – to the part where Mr. Benson takes his new boy to meet all his friends.

"Stroke book, eh?" Jack was, I could tell, amused.

I just said, "You've read it, I suppose."

"Read it? Honey, I'm sure you were still in junior high. For a while there, this character was everybody's role model – or dream daddy." Jack was fingering the teeth marks where one time I had bitten the book during an especially big come.

I blushed. "Well, that historical moment may be over for you, but the dykes have gotten hold of him now."

"I'm not even sure I can picture that," Jack said. He stroked his moustache absently. "You know, I have a few buddies of my own. But god knows, Randy, you'd embarrass me. You look like *baby* chicken when you're in drag."

I'D ALL BUT FORGOTTEN about that when I got a call from Jack on my voicemail. "Okay, Randy, I want you over here tonight at eight o'clock. Punctually. Butched up as much as your fey little ass can get. You won't need your girl drag, but bring your makeup."

I showed up at five minutes before eight and sat on the steps til it was time to ring the bell. I had on my engineer's boots and Levi's, and in a jockstrap I was packing a small one. My breasts were bound down and I had a worn black t-shirt under my leather jacket.

Jack answered the door. "Randy, for christ's sake, you look like a dyke."

"Jack, there's hardly any difference in this town!"

"Oh yes there is. Get in here, kid. You need a little more work."

Jack put me into a black leather bar vest that just fit me. He didn't tell me where it came from, but it was much too small for him. He asked me for my makeup kit. With its dark pencils and mascara brushes he darkened my eyebrows a little and stroked the fuzz on my upper lip with color until I had a moustache. "This stuff better be waterproof," he muttered. Finally he stood back and looked at me. "Where in god's name do you get boots that tiny? If only you were a few inches shorter. I could just tell them you're a dwarf."

"Jack, you're a total bitch. Who's 'them'?"

"Never mind, son. You'll see soon enough. Now drop to your knees, boy."

Happy to be back on familiar ground, I knelt with my cheek resting on Jack's thigh, filling with whatever the emotion was that his Daddyness brought up in me. An instant later I felt a chill coil of chain wrapping my throat and I started; Jack had never collared me before. At the click of the lock my cunt spasmed as if he'd flicked his tongue over my clit.

"You're my boy tonight, got it? You're going to keep your mouth shut and your jockstrap on. I'm upping the ante on our little social experiment, boy, and you're in it til it's over. No safe words, no femme drag, nothing but what I tell you. I'm taking you to a little party. You might just be the guest of honor." His eyes narrowed – I could see he was dead serious. "But if you don't keep up your end, you'll never be invited back – and I probably won't either. Don't fuck it up."

I stared up at him, welling up with the weirdest mixture of pride and stricken fear. I had only about a shred of an idea where we were going, but it was pretty clear Jack wanted me to pass on whomever we met. I had no idea how I was going to pull that off. I don't think I'd ever passed on anyone for more than about a half an hour in my life.

He put a blindfold on me before he handed me a helmet and straddled his Harley. I was left to grope my way on, and I held him tightly as the bike's acceleration threatened to knock me off balance. I tried, blind as I was, to follow the turns he took, but I was lost within a couple of blocks, and all I knew was that soon we were speeding up even more, crossing a bridge – I guessed the Bay Bridge, for in the middle the sound changed as we whipped through a tunnel. I clasped him, feeling the dildo I wore nudge his buttcheeks while his big bike throbbed under us like a very butch sex toy.

He didn't take the blindfold off until we'd entered a large house, which might have been in the Berkeley Hills, or Oakland, or who knows where. Jack had let himself in without ringing. We left our helmets on a shelf in the foyer. We weren't the only ones here, I noted: other helmets were there already, a briefcase or two, and a profusion of coats. Most, but not all, were leather. Jack instructed me to hang my own jacket on a hook – he always said it was too fucking ratty to be seen in – and kept his on. He led me down a long hall.

The room we entered at the end made me gasp. It was clearly a dungeon, though it was not the low-end made-over-basement I was used to from the city. Somebody well-to-do lived here, and he had obviously put all the care into constructing his playroom that some other gay man might spend collecting art or learning to be a four-star chef just to impress his friends.

At one end it didn't look like a dungeon, but a really classy den, a library without the bookshelves. It had several wing-back chairs arranged around a low table and facing a fireplace, where a small blaze flickered and cast shadows. A sideboard held a silver coffee service – a nice antique one, I noted – and several plates with sandwiches and other easy-to-eat food. A bottle of champagne lay icing in a silver bucket, but the cork hadn't been popped – no one seemed to be drinking. Three of the chairs were occupied by men in leathers, men who would look just as sexy and appropriate wearing very fine suits as they did in this Gentleman's Perv Club atmosphere.

The other end of the room was, like the part that looked like a den, wood-paneled. Wrought iron fashioned into cages and suspension bars set off the dark wood. A St. Andrews cross, leather-upholstered horses, and other dungeon implements furnished the place. I had been inside a few dungeons before, but they'd all looked tacked together compared to this.

As Jack stepped into the room, one of the seated men got up and extended his hand. Jack clasped it. "Sir Sebastian," he said, with affection as well as great respect in his voice, "how good to see you again. Thank you, as always, for your hospitality." Sir Sebastian, like Jack, had an impeccably trimmed beard, but it was mostly white, and he had white at the temples, too. I put him at fifty, perhaps, or a bit older. He was distinguished, calm, had seen everything. His grey eyes shone with warmth at the moment, but I could imagine them glittering menacingly; power was all over him. If Jack was my daddy, Sir Sebastian could be his.

"Jack, my darling man. You're welcome here at any time." He had looked me over once the moment we entered the room, and now he continued, "And what have you brought for us tonight? It's fortunate this isn't a public place, my dear. No wonder I haven't seen you in the bars with this lad."

Jack only smiled. "Sir Sebastian, his name is Randy. In my experience the name suits him very well, and he is not entirely new to all this. Tonight, of course, will be a test for him." As Jack said my name I sank to my knees and bowed my head. He hadn't told me what the rules were, except "don't fuck up"; I figured at the minimum I ought to put on good dungeon manners and hope I didn't miss any cues.

"Randy is forbidden to speak tonight," Jack said, "and I do hope none of you gentlemen will take offense when he does not verbally answer you. Also, his cock belongs to me, and neither he nor anyone else may touch it." I had a wild image of popping the little Realistic out of my jockstrap and handing it over to Jack for safe-keeping. "He is bandaged from a cutting, a rather extensive one, so I'd like you to leave his shirt on. Beyond that, however, he will be at your disposal."

At that my heart jumped wildly. Somehow I'd expected Jack to test my passing skills in a dark leather bar, not in a play-room full of masters. Why couldn't he have just snuck me into Blow Buddies? More was at stake tonight than whether I could keep the dildo on straight. I'm not a heavy sensation bottom, and while this place was beautiful, it could've hosted meetings of the Inquisition. I prayed I wouldn't break.

Jack ruffled my hair for the tiniest instant, then left me kneeling and turned to the other men. I stole glances up at them as best I could. One man was enormous and muscular, his head shaved, his tits pierced. I couldn't tell his age – somewhere around Jack's, perhaps. Jack called him Stone when he greeted him. He addressed another man, a lithe young blonde with icy blue eyes, as Marc. Marc seemed a good deal younger than the others, maybe even younger than me. But he wore authority like so many men in the bars wore leathers with the squeak and smell of Mr. S still on them.

Two more men came in. One was substantially older than the others, his hair quite white, and when he spoke I heard the tones of well-bred Oxford English. He, unlike the other men, did not wear leather; he was dressed in a suit that doubtless came from Savile Row. Jesus, Jack ran with some power daddies! "Ah, St. James, sir," Jack said when he saw the man, reaching to grasp his hand and, I noticed, inclining his head respectfully.

St. James' companion stepped forward to greet Jack, and at the sight of him I almost forgot to keep my head bowed. Tall, black, with sculptured muscles, he was one of the most beautiful men I'd ever seen. He had a similarly galvanizing effect on Jack. "Demetrius! How long have you been back?" he cried, and to my surprise threw his arms around the man. Demetrius laughed and hugged Jack, and even when the embrace was over they stood close, with their hands on each others' arms. I realized I was looking at someone who meant a lot to Jack – a lover, probably – and from my post on the floor I studied him as carefully as I could. He wore a white silk shirt which draped over his muscular arms and tucked into black leather pants almost as tight as his own skin. His fine leather boots were polished to a high black gloss. His voice was deep and smooth.

Sir Sebastian stepped to the sideboard and rang a small bell. A very pretty young man entered the room. He was dressed in a short jacket and tie, like a formal waiter, except he didn't have on any pants – only a leather jockstrap. His sandy hair curled around his face – he'd do flawless drag, I thought, then reminded myself that I probably wouldn't be let loose to play Barbie with Sir Sebastian's staff. Maybe Jack could get the loan of him sometime and we could play lesbians. He couldn't possibly have his obvious need to crossdress indulged hanging around with these leathermen.

The waiter-boy bore a tray with several champagne glasses. He set it on the sideboard and opened the champagne, not getting at all ostentatious with the cork, I noticed approvingly. It exited the bottle silently. He filled the glasses, presented one first to Sir Sebastian, then to St. James, and then to everyone else. He looked at me kneeling, poured a glass for me, and left it on the sideboard. "Anything further, Sir Sebastian?" he asked, and left silently when the man shook his head.

"Well, this is quite a lot to celebrate," Sir Sebastian said smoothly. "Jack has brought his new boy to meet us. And Demetrius has come back from his wanderings. Shall we toast?"

Jack picked up the glass from the sideboard and sat it on the floor in front of me, returning to lift his own glass. "New acquaintances and old friends," said St. James, and as the men all toasted I bent down and lapped from my glass like a rich old lady's over-indulged puppy. So far this party was a piece of cake, but that couldn't last. I repeated Sir Sebastian's statement, *Jack has brought his new boy,* in my head. Well, that was worth several hours of conversation about commitment and relationship status, eh? Jack's collar lay heavy on my neck, comforting as the touch of his palm on my nape. I stole another glance up through my lashes – he had his hand on Demetrius's strong, silk-clad shoulder, but I noted that he was reiterating to him and St. James the rules regarding my conduct. No speech – thank goodness; no removing my shirt, no touching my dick. Jack had done everything he could to set it up so I could pass.

44

Minutes later Jack was at my side, giving a lift to my collar. I scrambled to my feet, and at his gestured instruction, placed my hands behind my back at waist level. He beckoned and I followed – to the cage.

Inside the cage a set of leather cuffs dangled from chains. Jack adjusted them to my height, then held one open. Meekly I lay my wrist onto the fleece padding, and he buckled first that wrist in and then the other. The cage was tall enough for a full-sized man, but fairly narrow. Even with my wrists restrained, I could move right up to the bars on all four sides.

Jack took my chin, lifted my face up so I could gaze into his eyes. He was not quite expressionless – I thought I saw a hint of a smile. I figured that if we really pulled this off, Jack would feel like the cat that got the canary, and I – well, let's just say like the cat that ate the cream.

Then he released my chin and unbuckled my Levi's – the jeans fell down around my ankles. Jack slapped my ass once and grinned, then the cage door clanged shut; the lock snapped into place. He crossed the room and rejoined his friends.

"The devil never does get enough cock," Jack was saying. "He's a little pig, really. I think I've satiated the little bastard and ten minutes later he's pulling on my balls again. He's tiresome! I finally decided the only thing to do was bring him here." The assembled daddies murmured sympathetically.

"I'm sure we can help," Demetrius said.

"Oh, I know *you* can," Jack rejoined. "A cock like yours is really the only possible answer."

I listened to Jack with amazement. He was going to get me ganged! I rubbed my dick against the cage bars, felt my cunt simmer.

Sure enough, he returned accompanied by Marc. Each was unzipping his leather pants.

"Now, boy, I know I don't need to tell you to be good to my friends. You're here for our use. Take this."

Jack thrust his cock near enough to the cage bars that I

could just get to the pisshole with my tongue. I looked at him imploringly, the look that would have been accompanied by a "Please, Daddy!" if I'd been able to speak. Jack laughed and stepped closer, grasped the bars so he could press his pelvis right up against the cage, and his big cock came in for me to work on. I couldn't get hold of it with my hands – the restraints gave me some movement, but not enough – and so the only part of me that touched him was my mouth. I tongued him all over, the taste of him getting my saliva running, till his cock was wet and I could slurp him in. Marc stood just to one side of Jack, stroking his own cock – it had a downward curve, it would slide right down my throat.

"Look at this fucking cocksucker, Jack – where'd you find him? Look at this fucking kid." I knew how Jack liked it by now – he made a low little noise each time his cockhead slipped past my throat muscles, and when he pulled it out I laved my tongue all around the corona. Once in a while I let it slip out of my mouth so I could scramble for his balls – this part was harder with no hands, but Jack stayed close, his cock bobbing up to slap his belly with a soft *thwack* whenever its head escaped my lips. I could get only one of his nuts in my mouth at a time without the use of my hands – when my hands were free, I knew, if I opened really wide I could just get both of them in, and then I could suckle them. Now, though, I returned to his cock after a little attention to his balls, sucked him rhythmically, my tongue alert as it stroked along his shaft for the first pulsing signs of his load coming.

He didn't give it to me this time, though – gasping and swearing, he pulled out before I could finish him. Marc was in his place almost before I knew there was no cock in my mouth. His dick was a little longer than Jack's, maybe not quite as thick, but substantial, and with that downturn. "Little sucker," Marc growled, "you can have my load, punk, if you can work it out of me," and I went for him.

Demetrius and Stone stood a few feet back now, watching

too. As I breathed deeply, opened my throat, and started wiggling Marc's long curved one down as far as I could get it, Demetrius moved behind Jack and grasped his still-high cock in his big hand. Jack moaned, thrust into the fist like it was my cunt, started working it. When Marc's cock was all the way down my throat I started a fast gulping kind of suck. It flirted with my gag reflex, but I didn't care – that cock fit so perfectly in my throat, I didn't want to pull off it at all.

I was just about to drool from the saliva I wasn't bothering to stop and swallow when Marc started thrusting faster. This added movement pulled the long cock up and out, slid it back down and in, fast, hard, repeatedly, as the blonde man built up quickly towards his come. Jack was right on the edge of it too, but he wasn't missing a thing. "C'mon," he growled, "use that pig! Fill him up! Spray it right down his throat, man, that's what he's for!"

Marc bucked, knuckles white on the bars of my cage, and the next thrust I felt the first hot pulse of his jizz hit the back of my throat. Jack's dirty talk had the same effect on me it always did – added to the sensation of come spurting into me, filling my mouth up with bitter, creamy spunk, waves of come took me over, too. I could just reach the bars and I held on so I could keep on Marc's cock even as my come threatened to tumble me off my feet.

Stone had inched closer to the cage. Now the huge man snapped the codpiece off his chaps as he stepped up to take the place Marc vacated. Not only his head was smooth – Stone's cock and balls were shaved too, and a sizeable Prince Albert matched the rings that stretched out his nipples.

"Lick it up, little boy. Get it hard." Sucking in Stone's soft cock with the metal ring felt wild, and I suckled on it the way I liked to suckle Jack's balls. As it started to fill up he took it out of my mouth and, holding it, nuzzled it around my face, sometimes past my lips, sometimes under my chin. My whole face got slick from the sliding cock, and I hoped the fucking makeup on my upper lip was more than waterproof – I didn't think they behaved anything like this at the Max Factor test labs.

"Jack, I'm gonna fuck your kid, okay?" Stone slapped his almost-fully-engorged cock against my cheek.

"Sure, just get a rubber," said Jack.

Not an instant later the beautiful waiter-boy was at Stone's side, bearing a tray. Now where the fuck had he come from? I remembered that I'd heard Sir Sebastian's bell ringing a few minutes before. The boy must have come in then.

I could see his long pretty-boy meat outlined hard in his leather jock. I wondered if the help got to get laid around here, or what.

Stone picked a rubber off the tray, pulled it out of its wrapper, and worked it over his dick. The ring through his cockhead made the rubber fit a little funny, but I figured it'd probably work. Then he took a second one and repeated the process. While he suited up, Demetrius reached over Jack's shoulder and took a condom too.

I heard the sound of a zipper. Whose was that? Stone and Jack already had their cocks out. Then I heard Demetrius say, "Peaches, my pants, please," and the waiter knelt in front of him to help work the leather pants over his shiny boots. Peaches folded the pants carefully while Demetrius shucked the white silk shirt, then took them away. Over at the other end of the room, disguised by the woodwork, I saw a door swing open, and Demetrius' clothes went inside.

Stone, clad in rubber now, moved to the back of the cage. "Get your ass up here," he rasped. He reached through the bars to position me – there was just enough room for me to press my ass against the back bars and still be able to reach a cock fed to me at the front. Peaches reappeared silently, lube on his tray. Stone slathered up his cock, worked a finger into my ass. I shook with wanting this pierced-dicked giant to shove it in.

He didn't shove it, he worked it, and it felt so fucking good I could have screamed. I just grunted, low as I could pitch, and wiggled up onto him. "Jack, you're right, he's a fucking little pig," said Stone, "and I'm gonna fuck him just like one, ready, you little fuck, ready to get it jammed up your fucking pig butt?"

He had only arched into two or three hard thrusts when I felt my mouth opening again for cock – Jack's. I could have died of happiness. I sucked him down – *You want pig, Daddy, I'll show you what a pig you have* – and it was a minute before I noticed that Jack had shed his pants, too. Peaches stood near, still holding the tray which held the lube.

Then Demetrius, rubber on, started working his cock into Jack's asshole. Jack responded with a long groan, and I remembered that he'd been right up under an orgasm ever since I sucked him the first time. I backed off a little to give him time to get used to all the stimulation.

All four of us turned into a fucking machine, Stone and Demetrius pumping into Jack's and my butts simultaneously, me swallowing Jack's cock each time they did. We were all growling and all three of them were muttering, "Yeah. Fuck! Fuck your fuckin' ass, *fuck!*"

Thank god Jack's cock was too far down my throat when he started shooting to allow me any air to scream with – I was feeling like squealing, like the pig that I was, but his spasming cock kept me quiet. The minute he slid out of my mouth, all cummed out, he bent forward and sucked his jism out of my mouth. The kiss shut me up again when I was about to howl. The minute his mouth left me, there was Demetrius' cock, out of Jack's ass, rubber shed, at my lips.

His dick must have been as big around as my wrist – at least. It had the most prominent head on it I'd ever seen – though of course I couldn't see it right that minute. As it popped past the muscle at the top of my throat it burned, and I tried to shake my head, afraid I'd choke, afraid I couldn't. Stone, behind me and still riding me hard, saw. "Take that cock," he bellowed, giving my ass a stinging slap. "Take it, you fucking little punk!" I took it, seeing stars, stretching wider than I ever thought I could. Oh fuck, I thought, I'm playing with the big boys now.

Jack was back in commission. He was kneeling next to the cage, his face right next to mine, watching me growl and stretch to accommodate the thick meat. "Good boy," Jack murmured, "you're making me so proud, sucking that big hunk of cock. You can suck him, boy, you can get fucked by him, I know you want that, baby, don't you, can't get enough meat, hot little man."

That was it, wasn't it? I was where I'd always wanted to be, and I turned into a little demon, throwing my ass back on Stone's hard-pounding cock, suddenly finding room in my throat I didn't know I had. My hands clutched the bars for support and I worked both men for all I was worth.

"Chew on it." Jack was still right at my ear. "Chew that dick, boy. Don't worry about biting him, he likes it." I growled like a junkyard dog around Demetrius' substantial cock, chewing it like Jack told me to. Freed from cocksucking's one over-riding rule – *don't bite!* – I lost myself completely in the sensation of being filled up as full as I'd ever been. Thank god all the head I'd given already had filled my throat with that thick cocksucking slime – it lubricated even Demetrius' thickness. Stone pounded away behind me, and I had a feeling I knew how he'd earned his name.

But at last even Stone, who had been rhythmically fucking my ass for what seemed like an hour, started fucking even harder and faster. "Take it, you pig!" he grunted, really close to shooting, I could tell by his voice, and I felt Demetrius speed up too, both of them about to hose me, mouth and asshole, full of hot cream. "Comin'!" cried Demetrius. "Comin' right now!" And naturally I was shooting up the ramp right along with them, *I'd be a fine pig if I couldn't come right along with my tops, right, Daddy?* I opened my eyes to look at Jack, wanting to know he was seeing this, pumped full of his friends' jizz. I couldn't suck any more – my mouth was open as far as the muscles would stretch it, in a silent orgasmic yell – but that was okay, because the big man in front of me fucked my face now with pounding thrusts.

I REMEMBER THE FIRST HALF of the orgasm, but not the second.

I blacked out. I lost it, don't know exactly how it happened but it must have had something to do with my engorgable throat-flesh forming a seal with Demetrius' expanding, coming cock. I couldn't get enough air, I guess.

When I came to I had no idea where I was.

I felt damp clothes, chill air and motion, saw nothing but darkness, smelled the reek of not-quite-fresh piss. Where the fuck was I? A vehicle – a trunk? I felt around me in the utter black and yes, I was lying in a capacious car trunk, not bound, my leather jacket thrown over me, some kind of scratchy car blanket under my head, what felt like trash bags underneath my body. If I hadn't had such an extraordinary night, I'd have been terrified – but I was pretty sure this was part of Jack's buddies' idea of a good time.

The vehicle slowed, turned, turned again, and after a short distance stopped. I heard almost immediately the familiar sound of Jack's bike. Next, a car door slamming, then another. Two people? Then the trunk lid lifted.

It took a second for my eyes to adjust even to the dim alley light. We were outside Jack's place, back in the city. Jack and Demetrius stood there with a man I didn't know. He had on a driver's uniform, so I guessed that Sir Sebastian had lent the use of his car to get me out of there. What would a distinguished man like him do with a pissy piece of fucked-out chicken? After all. But had I pissed myself? It wouldn't have surprised me.

Demetrius reached into the trunk and lifted me like I was an unwieldy but not very heavy teddy bear. Jack had his keys out. The driver stood silently by. Sir Sebastian's help weren't a very talkative lot, were they? But at last, as Jack stepped up to the door, the driver said, "Shall I wait, sir?"

"Yes, do," said Demetrius, and he had me up the stairs and into the foyer.

"Here, let's clean the pig up," said Jack, gesturing Demetrius through his room and into the bath. He had the water running in the shower by the time we got there. Demetrius supported me while Jack stripped off my jacket, the bar vest, which I noted with chagrin was pissy too, and my boots and pants. He was about to thrust me under the hot spray with my shirt and jockstrap still on when Demetrius spoke up. "Go ahead, strip the girl down."

Jack and I both looked at him, eyes wide. I was stricken. I had been so exultant about passing! What gave me away?

Demetrius started to laugh, a low swell of a laugh that turned into a roar when he looked at me and saw my face. "Randy girl, you did good. I don't know what the fuck that was all about, but you pulled it off. No one else noticed a thing. I'm the one who carried you into the car, darling, and I took the liberty of feeling you up. Yes, I know your Daddy made a rule, but I've broken plenty of his rules before." At this Jack started laughing too. "Well, it's not like my meat hadn't just been all the way down your little throat. I felt further familiarities wouldn't be inappropriate. And your sweet little dick just seemed to come off in my hand. I tucked it back in, of course."

Jack was howling.

"I trust you have a bigger one than that, since you appear to be keeping Jack interested. I liked ganging Jack with you very much, dear, and I'd be glad to do that again any time you two want to give me a call. Jack, I'm back at my former number. Do phone me when you get time. I see we have more catching up to do than I thought. Randy – it's been a pleasure." With that, he gravely extended his hand, and as I took it I started laughing too.

Jack still laughed as Demetrius engulfed him in a bear hug – god, he was larger than Jack by almost as much as Jack outsized me – and I went ahead and shed the damp t-shirt and jock-strap and unwound the binding. As I stepped into the shower Demetrius took a look at me and said, "Sure enough, she's a girl, all right. Jack, you sick fuck! If St. James ever gets wind of this, he'll have his traditionalist boys come and turn your dick inside out. You and Little Bit here can go down to City Hall and register as domestic partners, and then you can spend your afternoons drinking coffee at the Whiptail Lizard Womyn's Lounge. You fucking wild man!"

Demetrius kissed Jack goodnight as I scrubbed the piss off. He ducked his head in the shower and kissed me too, and then he was gone.

Still grinning, Jack dried me off, capturing me for a minute in the big white fluffy towel. "Want some ice cream?" he said. "Good boys get ice cream."

"God, yes, I'm starving, Jack. I passed out before Peaches could come by with the sandwich tray."

Jack installed me in the flannel-sheeted bed, disappeared down the hall, and came back with two bowls. Before he started on his he stripped down, took a fast shower, and then joined me in bed. "Kid, you're more fun than a barrel of novices. You were terrific. I'm very proud."

I glowed as much from this as from the still very memorable fuck I still hadn't come all the way down from. The cold ice cream felt so intense on my throat that I almost squeaked. It was pretty sore from all that action. "Jack, I got piss on your bar vest. I'm so sorry. I don't know how it happened."

"No, *I* got piss on your bar vest. Leathers have to be broken in, child. We all doused you after you went out."

"What?"

"Sometimes it wakes people up," he said innocently. "Don't worry about going out, by the way. I think the first time I got down on that man's cock I passed out too. I was younger then, of course."

Then he told me what happened after I blacked out. I'd have fallen over but the men's cocks kept me suspended – Jack saw it as soon as it happened, though he let the guys finish coming. As first Stone and then Demetrius pulled their softening meat out of me, Jack reached into the cage to hold me up, and before he could even call for him, Peaches was there with the key, unlocking the cage door so Jack could undo my restraints.

"Jack, who were all those guys? Why didn't Sir Sebastian and St. James play? Didn't they like me?"

"Don't worry, honey. St. James loves this group of men, but he almost never plays. He's an old-timer. A traditionalist. He doesn't approve of the free-form way so many of us play now. I think he has a group of men he plays with back in London. He wouldn't be caught dead playing in a room with people who switch. Talk to him if you ever get a chance. Not many like him anymore. Sir Sebastian would have joined us if St. James hadn't been there, but he's too flawless a host to let a guest sit unentertained."

Jack snuggled me under his arm, the scent of which almost got me going again – but I was just too exhausted. I started to nod off to the sound of his murmurings, mostly of the "good little cocksucking pig" variety.

Right before I slipped under I whispered, "Thank you, Daddy" – and then, "Daddy, can we borrow Peaches?"

SPEAKER PHONE

Now that Demetrius had come back to town, I didn't see Jack for several days. Their reunion took all week. I spent a fair amount of time imagining what they might be up to – mostly this made me want to masturbate, and when I wanted to, most of the time I did.

I didn't feel jealous, particularly, though I missed Jack intensely. We didn't have the kind of relationship that lent itself to jealousy – in fact, we still hadn't talked about whether to call it "a relationship" at all. He'd collared me that last time, and we'd spent a lot of nights together, and we talked on the phone a lot. In the absence of the flesh-on-flesh Jack I missed, wanting to stay connected, I'd left them phone messages almost every day. Jack had left me some in return.

In his last message he said, "Randy, be home tonight at eight. We'll be calling." Kind of cryptic: I wasn't sure whether "we" was Jack and Demetrius, though I assumed so, and it wasn't clear whether "calling" meant phone calling or *come* calling. I straightened my room up just in case it was the latter, though Jack rarely came to my house. I was showered and dressed in my good jeans, boots and a pressed white shirt with one leather lace knotted around my throat like a tie, presentable in case anyone arrived to present myself to.

The phone rang at eight on the dot. I got it on the second ring, eager to hear Jack's smoky, sexy voice.

"Hi, piglet," he said. "Don't say anything. Do what I say. Put it on speaker phone."

I almost fucked up right away by saying "Okay, Jack," or "Yes, sir," but I caught myself. I did as he instructed: hit the speaker phone button and put the receiver gently down.

"Good girl," he said, when he could hear by the change in the phone's sound quality that I'd followed his directions. "Now get on your bed and just listen."

I recognized Demetrius's voice, deep and smooth. "This sexy man isn't wearing any clothes at all," he said, "except his boots." Jack laughed. "You know the way his cock curves up just a little when he's hot? Well, it's doing that now."

I knew, indeed. When that cock slipped inside me, the upcurve rubbed me very right.

"Course, I'm helping it a little," Demetrius continued. *I'll bet you are*, I thought. "Tell your Miranda girl what I'm doing to your cock, Jack."

"He's got my cock and balls tied up in about six feet of leather lacing," Jack informed me. "The skin on my balls and shaft is shiny and tight and turning purple. It feels unbelievable."

"You can do better than that, Jack. Describe the way it feels."

A light slap sounded in the background and I heard Jack let his breath out. He was silent for a second. Then he said, "Like a balloon inflating to the point that it feels like it will burst. Hot and tingly, and cold at the same time. Super-sensitive."

"That's better," Demetrius said. "That's exactly the way it feels when I'm tied up like this." Several more tiny slap sounds later, Jack was breathing hard; I pictured his big lover the way I'd seen him first, earring gleaming against his dark skin, creamy silk shirt billowing, black leather pants tight. If he was topping Jack – and it sure sounded that way so far – he'd still be dressed while Jack stood before him naked, seeming more vulnerable without his leather jacket, his chaps, his perfectly worn jeans. I wondered where they were calling from; I wanted the picture I was conjuring in my mind to have as much detail as if I were in the room watching them.

"Jack, put your hands up to the bar." What bar? They weren't at Jack's place, then; there wasn't anything like a bar there. "I have a suspension bar here, Miranda" – Demetrius spoke as if he had read my thoughts – "and I'm about to put Jack into cuffs." I heard some movement and rustling, though nothing that gave me a clear picture, as the cuffs went around Jack's wrists and were buckled closed – but the picture of Jack with his arms lifted high, naked in his boots with his hard cock tied into a tight harness, forced a moan out of me, one loud enough for the men to hear over the speaker phone.

"Jack, before I get on with my business, I think you'd better make sure your girl is behaving herself," said Demetrius.

"Randy, what are you doing? Are you playing with yourself while you listen?"

I stayed silent for a beat too long, because Jack had told me not to talk. I didn't want to break his rule, even though he'd asked me a direct question. While I was trying to think my way out of the dilemma he laughed, recognizing why I hadn't spoken. "Permission to speak granted," he said. "Are you masturbating, Randy-girl?"

Whew. "Um, no, Jack," I said, "though the thought was starting to cross my mind."

"As is only natural," put in Demetrius.

"Yeah, I suppose I'd be offended if you hadn't thought about it," Jack said, "but keep your hands to yourself til I say you can jerk off. As easily as she comes," he explained to Demetrius, "she'd be twenty or thirty orgasms ahead of us before we get around to getting off."

"Can't have that," said Demetrius. "So Randy, the rules are, no masturbating til we say. Understand?"

"Yes, sir," I replied, feeling suddenly like I had two lovers instead of one. I tried putting my hands between my thighs to keep them unoccupied, but in just a few seconds I realized that this was practically masturbation, even when I tried to keep very still. They pressed against my mons and clit, and trying to adjust them so they didn't felt even more like masturbation, so I removed them and lay with my arms down at my sides. It felt unnatural, but then, this whole situation was on the unnatural side. In a very good way.

A mysterious set of sounds came from the speaker phone, just a little indistinct, so it took me a while to figure out what I was hearing. I finally worked it out: more of the light slaps I'd heard before, combined with the wet slurps and occasional tiny squeaks of sucking; Jack's breath, steady in and out but a little heavier than he usually breathed. I figured that Demetrius was sucking Jack's nipples – it wasn't Jack doing the sucking, his breathing was too even – and continuing to slap his bound cock. When Jack's breath got ragged or especially deep, it meant Demetrius had used his teeth.

Soon the breath was more ragged than not. More and more teeth, I guessed. Jack had great nipples for sucking or biting – firm, erect, bigger than most men's. Sometimes he told me to close my teeth around them and pull, pull steadily. I could feel his nipple ring click against my teeth, tease it with my tongue. He took an amazing amount of this, and sometimes he even came that way.

"Your daddy's nipples are standing out like raspberries, Miranda," said Demetrius. "Stiff engorged berries. I'm going to clamp them now." After the faint rattle of chain and two matched gasps, one after the other, he continued, "And now I'm going to pull this chain out as far as I can. See how he likes it." Jack seemed to like it a lot; he started to groan. I wondered why Demetrius hadn't just threaded a thong through Jack's rings; maybe he wanted to give him the extra sensation of the clamps.

"My, my, Jack," – Demetrius punctuated this with a couple of slaps – "it's a mighty lot of work to pull on these chains myself. A man has to exert himself to get you properly worked over." I stifled a giggle. "Let's just attach them to your wrist cuffs, so I can let go of them. That's it." A louder groan, as he pulled Jack's nipples far enough for the chains to reach. I heard the click of a clip snapping onto one cuff's D ring. Then the other.

"Let's see – what else is in this bag?" Demetrius rummaged around, clanking chain. "Oh, this is good. Very good."

Two more gasps, the kind of sounds Jack had made when the nipple clamps went on. Then I heard a hum that escalated rapidly to a high-pitched buzz. A vibrator? Jack's breathing changed again, almost at once – it stayed ragged, though I could hear him fight to slow it. He was trying to control his arousal. Did Demetrius have a vibrator on Jack's cock? I'd never used one with him. This was too, too hot.

"Miranda, I've got Jack in a set of vibrating clamps. One end is clipped to a fold of skin I pinched up from his perineum. It's not quite on his asshole, but it's close." I tried to picture it, hanging like an egg behind his balls, buzzing relentlessly. What would that feel like? "I've got the other end clipped right below his cockhead. That spot of his that's so sensitive, you know?" Jack's gasps had my clit buzzing as hard as Demetrius' devilish little toy, straining as hard as Jack's bound, beautiful cock. I feared I'd have one of those rare no-hands orgasms just from listening and picturing Jack tied up, his body an arc from the soles of his boots to the place where his wrists were bound, above and a little in front of him. His nipples stretched out like a sundancer's and his cock full, purple and throbbing.

"Miranda, do you have a vibrator there with you, dear?" For that matter, Demetrius's voice was enough to make me come. "One of those wand things, what do you call them?"

"Magic Wands. Yes," I said, my voice sounding funny, and no wonder – I hadn't breathed for what seemed like minutes.

"Jack, boy, would you like to tell your girl to go ahead and come? Maybe the two of you can come at the same time. That would be so romantic."

Jack's voice sounded pretty funny too. He had to speak slowly because of the way he was tied and because of the buzz that relentlessly brought him up towards orgasm. "She... comes...fast...with...that....thing, sir."

"Doesn't matter," said Demetrius. "You're gonna come pretty quick yourself once my cock slides up your hole, Jack."

Oh my fucking god. I reached for my vibrator as stealthily as I could. Condom-wrapper sounds masked any rustling noise that might have given me away. I knew I couldn't get away with switching the wand on until Jack told me to, but when that moment came I didn't want to miss a nanosecond of insistent, buzzing stimulation. I pictured Demetrius' thick cock, rubbered up now, nudging Jack's cheeks apart. The vibrator rested on my clit like a horse at the gate, just waiting for the gun.

"Here goes, Randy," said Demetrius. "I've got your daddy's hands tied up as high as he can reach and still be on his feet. His tits are clamped up there too. His cock is trussed up tight, and I've got the clamps on his cock and his taint. I'm standing behind him. I've got my rubber on and my cock lubed up real good. I know what he can take better than he does. When I get him by the hips and pull him back, he'll be off balance and on my cock. He doesn't have any choice at all."

Jack – and I – both moaned at this, though the thought that Jack would want anything other than Demetrius' cock sunk ballsdeep into him was, frankly, ridiculous. Jack lived to be butt-fucked. Hog heaven was just around the corner.

"I've got my dickhead pressed right up against his asshole, Randy-girl. Tell her, Jack – now!"

"Go!" Jack's command started out as a bark and ended as a deep, guttural groan. That meant he was suspended on Demetrius' meat, impaled, balanced on it like he was floating in air. Before the last "uh!" was out of him, my vibrator started humming along with the higher-pitched buzz of the nipple clamps. Right away my body took on an arc like Jack's, not from tight bondage but from the force of the vibration on my clit. It hit me like a truck. I had never been so ready to come – at least, not without any physical foreplay.

I imagined what it would be like suspended in front of Jack right now, his cock in my ass the center of all that I could feel or know, with Demetrius' hard thrusts into Jack's hole the only motion that thrust him into me. I imagined Demetrius himself splitting my cheeks, his cock huge, big around as my wrist, fucking himself deeper and deeper into me – just as, this minute, he fucked himself into Jack. I knew this because of the rhythm of both men's breath, coming out in huffs and shouts and gasps in time to Demetrius' thrusts. I saw Jack's cock even more tight and purple as it got more and more engorged. I saw his asshole stretched and filled by Demetrius' meat. My head thrown back, my hips arched up, I fucked my clit into the strong buzz of the vibrator. My breath caught in my throat now like it always does when I climb up to a come, especially a really big one, and like always I imagined Jack's hand around my throat, cutting off my air. Demetrius huge in my ass like he really was right now in Jack's and Jack's hand squeezing tighter threatening to black me out and the men's fuck sounds in my ear and Jack's fingers invading my cunt now where he could feel Demetrius' meat through the cuntwalls and stroking it and making Demetrius fuck me faster harder ramming in and bringing me up too high to stop and then finally – in the clear second before I came, before I started yelling my out-of-control come along with theirs – I saw Jack before me looking into my eyes, steely blue deep into my heart, my cunt, everything.

We really all three came at the same time. Demetrius' *"Coming!"* came out a cross between a shout and a groan. I knew by the time he fucked his load into the rubber that he had Jack by the nipples, using the engorged, clamped bits to pull Jack over and over onto him. Jack growled, animal sounds that wouldn't let my orgasm stop. Over the hum of my vibrator I finally heard the sound of chains clinking, buckles coming undone, the high buzz of the vibrating clamps cease as Demetrius took Jack down. Footfalls on the wooden floor accompanied my last orgasm, and after it was over Jack's voice came, closer now, "Enough, slut." Even though it had very little edge – Jack's top space was lost up his butt for the time being – I obeyed him, switching off the wand, curling up facing the speaker phone. I imagined Demetrius curled up around Jack. I imagined them on their sides on Demetrius' bed, and for a moment I felt very alone. All I could hear was their breath.

"Well, Randy" – Demetrius broke the silence – "that was really strangely intimate." I chuckled a little. "I was quite aware of your presence with us, in spite of the fact that you might not even be in the same area code right now."

"She's about three blocks away, Demetrius," said Jack, voice all whiskey and honey with the effects of being fucked into the middle of next week.

"Three? Is that all, boy?"

Jack said "*Mmm hmm*."

"Are you dressed, Randy?"

I said I was. I hadn't actually even opened my jeans to buzz. All that sensation, right through the denim.

"This is too excellent. So often you have to fuck up afterglow if you want anything." Demetrius told me the address, just off Polk Street. "Ice cream, chocolate, two pints. Bowls in the kitchen. Oh, and draw a bath on the way in."

I tucked in my shirt on the way to the door. The speaker phone buzzed for a minute. Then silence.

THE OLD DAYS

I thought Jack and Demetrius might want to play with me when they called me over, but it turned out that Demetrius really did want me primarily as an ice cream slave. I showed up with a couple of pints of Double Rainbow and got bowls and spoons from the kitchen. They were cuddled up in bed, sure enough, though after I served them ice cream they made room for me in the middle. I took off my boots and jeans and crawled between them. This position made me dangerously squirmy, actually, because both men were so fucking hot I could barely keep my hands off their dicks. But they'd played already, and they weren't sending out signals that they wanted to play any more.

I didn't feel like eating ice cream so much as spooning some on my clit to cool it down. I figured a little story telling might distract me.

"So tell me about the old days," I said. "Tell me what the baths were really like."

"The old days!" Demetrius laughed. "It's come to that, Jack. This little upstart makes it sound like we're in the same league as her grandfather."

"Hardly!" I protested. "Demetrius, I didn't mean it that way!"

"Course not, baby, but remember, those days are sort of out of our reach, too. Around these parts, anyway."

I really was curious about what made a bathhouse differ from a sex club. I had actually sneaked into clubs more than once while in drag, though I could never relax completely when I did – too afraid of getting found out. I used to feel safest at the Blow Buddies, where I could hide in a cubicle with a glory hole and suck cock all night. Until they instituted a dick check at the door, that is. I couldn't very well pull my Realistic out of my jockstrap and plunk it down on the counter next to my admission fee. Rumor had it another woman in drag got caught one night, which is why they started this new policy.

"There are still sex clubs around," I said.

"Not the same," said Jack at once.

"Nope, not the same," said Demetrius.

"Well, why not? What was different?"

"'In the old days,'" Demetrius mocked, but sweetly.

"In the old days," Jack began, "there were baths all over the city. Some were really deluxe, with beautiful facilities – steam and sauna, sometimes even a pool, and often a place to get something to eat. A few of them, like the Continental, had full-on entertainment. Some very famous people got their start there."

"Ever get to the Continental in New York when Bette Midler played there?" asked Demetrius.

"Yeah, a couple of times."

"I know guys who worked there back then."

"I'm surprised you guys didn't meet there," I said. I knew they'd been lovers for a long time, but not 25 years.

"Who knows, maybe we did," said Jack. Demetrius snickered. "It got pretty dark in certain areas," Jack went on, "though I swear, baby, if this cock had ever done what it did to me earlier this evening, I'd have just followed you home."

"That's exactly what happened in real life, Miranda," Demetrius said, "except it wasn't at the baths, it was later, at a leather party. He was the sweetest little puppy once, your Daddy."

Jack snickered this time. "Back to the baths," he said.

"Oh, don't I wish!" sighed Demetrius. "Now, Randy, they weren't all classy, you understand. Don't get all fixated on the picture of dozens of fags in white towels gazing up at Bette

Midler – charming though that picture is, in retrospect. Instead, envision a steam room full of naked men, hot fog swirling around them. Think of an orgy room so dark you don't know whether the man you're fucking is black or white. Picture a hallway of open doors, and behind each door a naked man on a towel, showing you his ass."

"Picture a sleazy neighborhood – because that's the only part of town the baths could locate," added Jack. "Picture a Mafia-owned place where you'd be asked no questions about who you were. We got away with wild sex and hard drugs 'cause it was all illegal to start with. It could be in a SOMA alley or a dock in the meatpacking district, right off the Hudson. Picture a place where if somebody passed out – too many drugs or too much excitement – he'd get dragged outside and left for the cops to find."

"Yeah, they'd call the cops anonymously so he wouldn't have to stay out there too long. And it was a real secret fraternity. You could run into your local alderman there and nobody would say anything about it. It was underground the way nothing is today. You couldn't find the baths unless you were in the life," said Demetrius. "Picture a hallway with a line of men leaning against the wall. A *long* hallway. A *lot* of men."

"And imagine a time when it didn't matter if you fucked bareback all night," Jack added, "and you weren't going to catch anything you couldn't just visit the clinic to get rid of."

"I met one of my dearest old boyfriends in line at City Clinic," said Demetrius. "We figured out we must have had the exact same strain of clap. I think we both got it at the Bulldog Baths. Probably from the same guy."

"I loved the Bulldog," Jack said. "Remember the mural?"

"Everything going on in that mural went on in the back room," said Demetrius. "Sucking, fucking, fisting, guys getting tied up. And the mural had a bulldog on it, too. Fucking some guy's ass."

"Hey, I've seen that!" I said. "I think it was in the Gay and

Lesbian Historical Society newsletter!"

"Historical," Demetrius growled. "There she goes again, Jack."

"The guys on the mural reminded me of the Village People."

Demetrius groaned out loud at that. "The Village People!" he said. "*Indeed!*"

"Some of the men at the baths actually *were* construction workers, Miranda," said Jack. "Butch men were very much in demand, especially if they lived the life. Cops were very popular. Truckers. You get the picture."

"Like 'El Paso Wrecking Company.'"

"More or less."

I had to admit I was playing just a little dumb – the better to bring out the details. I knew full well the men in the Bulldog mural had nothing to do with pop faggery. They were the real deal.

"Also popular," mused Demetrius, "was a guy I used to see at various bathhouses and also at the Ambush, which had such a famous back room that it practically counted as a bathhouse itself. This guy was a thalidomide child, I suppose. His arm ended in a hand with only one finger. It was just a perfect taper. Naturally you can imagine the men lining up. He was an ideal date for the man who'd never been fisted."

"Like a training bike."

"You little snot." Demetrius burst out laughing. "Yeah, something like that. He'd show up elsewhere too, sometimes, but the Ambush was really his home. You could walk up to the bar and ask for poppers as easily as you could buy a beer."

"I remember that," said Jack. "There was a fridge in front of the bar just full of poppers. Real good ones. This predated that butyl crap by years. Real amyl – the back room smelled of it all the time."

"And Crisco."

"Fucking A, and Crisco. You can't get that smell out."

"The Castro had barely begun to go queer when I first hit town, Randy," said Jack. "On Halloween night they closed off a stretch of Polk Street. It was just as wild then as Castro is now.

Wilder, because there weren't any tourists. Everybody went there to party. They let fourteen-year-olds into some of the bars. It was still illegal to do drag. When those queens hit the streets, they had to be ready to fight off the cops. It was that way before and after Stonewall. Here we faced off the cops at a drag ball in 1965. And they act like the queens at Stonewall gave birth to the whole world."

"Drag was illegal?" Now I *did* feel naive.

"Fuck, yes," said Demetrius. "You couldn't be wearing more than two pieces of women's clothing. I guess this was supposed to spare the poor fool who had to wear his sister's sweater to go down to the corner store, or something. But when drag queens dressed, they always knew it could be trouble. Course, everything everyone did was illegal before the consenting adults law passed."

"We weren't adults anyway," Jack said with a laugh.

"Well, *you* weren't," said Demetrius. "As your little friend reminds us, though, Jack, we're antiques now."

"Please," I said. "*Brady Bunch lunchboxes* are antiques now. How do you think that makes *me* feel?"

"Once I'd graduated from high school," Jack said, "there was nothing to stop me from going to the baths all the time. Eventually I had to get a job, but for a while I was in the door when they opened and sometimes I didn't leave til they closed. All I needed was a nickel pack of K-Y to get me started. After that, each one's load made it slick for the next one."

"A butt slut, Miranda. Would you ever have guessed? Darling, you must have been a true hazard once you finally got to the shower. Leaving a snail trail like that on the wet tile."

"What were you into, Demetrius?" I asked.

"As many of those butts as I could get, baby," he said. "Best of all, I liked the orgy rooms. When they had any light at all – which was rare – it felt like I was living in decadent old Rome. A butt would come sliding back towards my dick and I'd think, 'Render unto Caesar that which is Caesar's.'"

"What a *queen!*" Jack's tone held nothing but admiration.

"But I liked it better when there wasn't any light at all. You had to do everything by feel. Like I said, you couldn't tell black from white there, or any other color. Learned a lot from that. The rest of the damned world could use more of what those orgy rooms had."

I tried to imagine being in a dark-as-pitch room full of writhing, fucking people. My strategy for staying distracted wasn't working – I wanted to writhe and fuck, myself.

"There was even a mixed bathhouse, Randy. The Sutro. You could have gone, if you'd been around then."

"Lord have mercy! She would have given the fags a run for their money, Jack."

"She still does."

"Did either of you ever go there?" I asked.

"Only out of curiosity," said Jack. "I wasn't doing women in those days."

"I went a few times before they closed. Liked it, but it was different from the all-male places."

"Because of the women?"

"I used to think so, but now I'm not sure. Now I think the difference was more likely the straight men who were there for the women. They weren't all this way, but some of them definitely just didn't understand that at an open sexual space like that, there would be men who were into men and women who were into women. They acted like the queers were invading their space, when really it was more like the other way around."

"I know what you mean," I said, having run into such guys at sex parties. "Plus they act like every woman is there to fuck them. They think a woman who is sexually free is available no matter what."

"Make 'em pay for it," sighed Demetrius. "It's the only way to regulate them. We had trolls in the baths, too, and honey, when god handed out social skills, those guys were in the bathroom jerking off. They're kids who didn't know they were supposed to bring a penny to go to the candy store."

"This just gets me thinking," said Jack. "We should take Randy with us to Blow Buddies next week."

"But they do a dick check!" I cried.

"Now, how would you know that?" asked Demetrius. "No, wait. Don't tell me. Let me guess. One of those humorless old queens confiscated your penis the last time you tried to sneak in."

JACK'S WILDEST TIME: TEACUP TOY

"What's the most outrageous adventure you ever had?" Jack asked one morning over breakfast.

"Meeting you."

"But before that."

"I'll tell you mine if you tell me yours."

"Deal."

"I USED TO SPEND a lot of time at the Ambush," Jack began.

"When was this, the '70s?" I knew the Ambush hadn't been around for a long time.

"Yes, remember what Demetrius and I told you? When they kept their poppers in a big fridge, and after you bought them you could go upstairs and use them right away."

"My earliest memories of gay bars have men doing poppers while they danced."

"Amateurs," Jack snorted. "At the Ambush you went upstairs and got fisted. Or into the men's room to give head or swallow piss."

"I'll bet there wasn't even a ladies' room," I said, saucily.

"Good point. There most certainly was not."

"So what happened there that was so wild? Besides everything."

"Well, one night I went in and there was a hot man at the bar whom I hadn't seen before. I hadn't been going there for too long – I'd been out for a while, but I was just getting into the kind of sex you went to the Ambush for."

"You mean one time you used to be a sweater boy?"

"Shut up, Miranda."

"Sorry. Tell me a story, Jack."

"So this guy, when I got closer to him, turned out to have a little dog with him. I think it was a Chihuahua, but it was a pretty studly one. Maybe it was crossed with one of those little tiny Dobermans. Anyway, the guy had this dog in a little leather bar vest –"

"Like the kind you got me?"

"Just exactly like that. Only smaller. And he had a little shot glass of beer for the dog, while he drank a big schooner. Well, you know what they say about dogs. They're a great way to meet people. I walked right up and sat down and introduced myself. I knew just enough not to say 'Cute dog.' Good thing, too, 'cause this man took his little dog very seriously. He introduced him to me as Spike."

"*Très* butch!" I said. "Did the guy have a name?"

"Yeah, Mike."

"You're making this up!"

"I am not, Miranda! But I know it sounds like a figment. Okay, Mike was truly hot, even if he did have this butched-out rat dog with him. So one thing led to another and I asked him if he wanted to go into the back room. But he said no, it was too dangerous for Spike to go back there. It was always so dark in the back rooms, and he didn't want to lose sight of the little guy and get him stomped.

"But he said he'd love to take me home."

"You went, right?"

"Of course I went. I figured when we got there Mike would let Spike out of his drag and the mutt would go chew on a little rubber bone or something. But we got to his place, it turned out he had something real different going on."

"Different how?"

"He was carrying the dog inside his leather jacket on the way home – any time Spike didn't like the looks of someone passing by, he'd stick his head out of Mike's coat and growl like a little motherfucker. Looked like an alien. When we got to Mike's place, the dog went right onto the bed. He waited there while Mike and I got into it, getting into each other's clothes, getting 'em off. He was an amazingly hunky man, with a couple of days' beard growth that rasped me when we kissed – he was some kisser – and big tits with rings. That was before I was pierced. I really got into pierced tits. It turned out his cock was pierced too."

"With a Prince Albert?" I liked PAs.

"No, not a PA – it didn't go through his urethra at all. It was an ampullang, I think. Most men wear a bar in theirs, but this guy wore a ring. A pretty intense piercing. My hands found it before I saw it, when my hands went into his Levi's before I pulled them off him. I found that so fucking hot, feeling him up and my fingers touching steel."

I nodded. I found it hot too.

"Once we were undressed, he pulled me toward the bed. I thought we were going to get into it, but he said, 'Watch this,' and pointed to the end of the bed like he wanted me to sit down there. So I did. The minute he was on the bed, the little dog was right on him."

"What do you mean?" I had seen a couple of photo books from Amsterdam, so I knew stuff with a dog was possible – but those dogs were huge. "What could a Chihuahua do?"

"Plenty! First he grabbed Mike's ring, the one in his dick, with his teeth. He growled and shook it – like when a dog gets a rat, you know? Or in his case a mouse, I guess, since he was only rat size himself. He worried Mike's cock and the guy got harder and harder. Really big dick, too. Picture it – juicy big fucking cock, pierced, with this little dog in a bar vest giving him a hard-on instead of me."

"Were you pissed off or anything?"

"No, because it was too weird and fascinating. It was hot, actually, and I had never seen anything like it, and I got off on watching it.

"So Spike gave Mike a big hard one, and while that was going on, I noticed, the dog's cock got erect too – a little glistening red spike between his tiny little haunches. Maybe that's how he got his name. What do you think happened next?"

I couldn't quite imagine. I was thinking of the very big glistening red prongs on the dogs in the Amsterdam pictures. Maybe Mike could suck his little dog off, but the hotness factor of that kind of escaped me – though it would still make a good bizarre story. If I was going to suck a dog off, I didn't think I'd go for a teensy one, and I really didn't think that was what a big leatherfag would go for.

"Spike suddenly let go of Mike's ring," Jack continued. "He was standing on the bed, of course, and Mike's legs were spread wide to let the dog get to his cock. When Spike let go, the hard-on slapped up to Mike's belly – he was incredibly hard by then, and his erection was as tight as any I'd ever seen. And the dog jumped up on his belly and began humping Mike's cock. His little paws grabbed Mike's cock, and I watched him aim that slick red dog dick and sink it right into Mike's pisshole."

"No!"

"Yes – but for a minute I couldn't believe it myself. I got right up next to this scene. I swear, I saw it with my own eyes, eight inches away."

"How big was this dog's cock?" I asked.

"Maybe two inches long or a little longer. Big around as a pen. The guy's urethra was definitely big enough. I've seen guys who've played with sounds who can take my index finger up their piss slits. This little dog dick was nothing compared to that."

"Yeah, except there was a *dog* attached!"

"A madly humping dog attached. He was going for it. You ever see dogs fucking?"

"Yeah, plus when I was in high school my best friend's poodle used to have a real thing for my Reeboks."

"So you know how fast they can go. But after a while they stop. I thought he was done, but Mike got all orgasmic, like – like when guys get fisted, and they come, but without ejaculating."

"Like when *I* come, Jack. There's really no difference."

"He was coming like that. He told me afterward that the dog's cock swells up inside whatever it's fucking, so it was the size of a grape inside his cock, stuck inside, and the little dog was pumping come into him. Up his urethra. It went on for quite a while. Mike was all swoony and hot over it. The rat dog was pretty swoony too, come to think of it. He finally finished coming and his dick came out of Mike's slit with a little pop. Then he curled up on the pillow next to Mike's head, licked the end of his dick, and went to sleep."

"Sweet! What did you do, suck Chihuahua come out of your new pal's meat?"

"Well, yeah, eventually," Jack said, grinning. "But that scene with Spike just got him started. He was wild, that guy. I told him he should get a matching Great Dane so he could get it from both ends. I wouldn't be surprised if he took my advice."

"Fabulous!"

Now the story was getting really interesting. Whatever it is about small dogs, I just can't get turned on to them. Thinking about Spike in action was the closest I'd ever gotten to seeing a little dog as sexy. "Jack, there's a Dane that I saw last year at the Castro Street Fair – he was with a leatherman. Could that be Spike's new big brother?"

"Maybe," said Jack. "But this was years ago, and I haven't seen Mike around for a long time. I wouldn't be surprised to hear he'd inspired other guys with his tastes, but I sure as hell haven't seen another hunk toting around a Chihuahua."

MIRANDA'S WILDEST TIME: CLUB CLITOSAURUS

"What about your wildest story?" asked Jack.

I told him about the time Ariel and I took her drag queen friends Mari and Yvette to Club Clitosaurus. It was a lesbian sex club in the SOMA warehouse of a punk dyke band. They usually rehearsed there, but every once in a while they'd clean it up, throw sheets over the vintage 1963 furniture, and have a party.

Mari and Yvette were convinced they were lesbians. Ariel told me that they would have started a transgender process long ago, except that they also liked being fags so much. So most of the time they dressed as boys – deeply cute ones, at that – and went to ACT-UP demos to vent their spleen and cruise. But when they crossdressed they were totally lesbian identified, and ever since Ariel had started living full time as a woman they'd been after her to sneak them into women's clubs. She'd taken them to plenty of lesbian bars, and they actually passed a little better than she did, because Ariel was so tall. Yvette and Mari were both very small men. Mari didn't even need to shave. Mari kept trying to get Yvette to accept the fact that Yvette was the more butch of the two, but Yvette wasn't having any of it; he had grown his hair out especially so he could pass better.

I said that they were obviously both very femme lipstick lesbians and that Ariel and I would be the butches.

It took us at least two hours to get ready to go. The blinking neon light outside Ariel's Tenderloin apartment always put me in the mood for queer urban slumming, and that night seemed queerer than most. Between them, Mari and Yvette had enough makeup to stock a department store cosmetics counter, and they'd each brought a suitcase of clothes along. They wanted me to dress them appropriately, since I was the only one who'd been to Clitosaurus. I loved playing Barbie with fags, but I was at a loss over one thing.

"What are you going to do about your dicks?" I asked.

Even Ariel had one, of course. She was pre-op – "or maybe non-op, I haven't decided yet," she'd say – and I was a little worried about being the one to bring a trio of cocks into a dyke inner sanctum like Clitosaurus. Ariel really wouldn't be a problem, since she was on hormones and people knew she identified as a dyke, but I didn't know how the Clitosaurus dykes would take the boys – er, the girls.

"Don't you know about gaffs?" Ariel asked. She showed me how the special garment allowed their cocks to be tucked away out of sight, leaving nothing more telltale than a soft mound of what might be pussy. Mari and Yvette bound their cocks back, too.

That problem out of the way, it was time to play dress-up. "Okay, no drag queen makeup," I instructed. "Be just a trifle subtle." So they stopped at dark red lipstick and not-too-over-the-top eyeliner – certainly nothing more ostentatious than the drag queen wannabe femmes would be sporting at Clitosaurus.

The girls both had expensive, grabbable fake breasts that fit perfectly into the cups of a bra. Mari's went into a lacy black bra, Yvette's into a leather one. Mari had fishnets, red Doc Martens, and a black velvet minidress. I dressed Yvette in black leather pants and high heels, and Ariel french-braided his thick blond hair. They both had black leather jackets – just like everybody else at the party would have – and, dressed, standing in the neon pulse, they looked like a couple of killer femmes. Ariel and I were pleased.

"Call a cab," I said.

I had reserved for four at Clitosaurus. I told Margy, who always held down the door, that Mari and Yvette were my friends from out of town, and that Ariel was my new girlfriend. That much, at least, was true. Margy, a rangy butch, eyed the girls appreciatively. I could feel Mari squirm under her blue–eyed scrutiny. I had my feelers out for matches I could make; I knew that in this crowd there'd be at least a few women who'd find Mari and Yvette's equipment something like a wacky new type of strap-on. With the right introductions, the girls would fit right in, and it wouldn't even matter if someone noticed they were boys. I would have no problem entertaining them myself, if it came to that.

"C'mon, I'll show you around," I said as we passed Margy's station. Before us was an open room, topped on three sides by a balcony. Stairs led up, and women lounged around the railings, watching what went on below. Downstairs was mostly dungeon, with a row of slings suspended on the far wall under the balcony overhang. We walked upstairs first, where the old furniture had been arranged in groups – a sofa or two, a flat square '60s armchair – upon which women in twos and threes lounged, making out or watching the few who had already begun to play.

"Want to watch or be watched?" I whispered. A long L-shaped sofa stood empty.

"Both."

"Ever lick pussy, baby?" I said to Yvette. Ariel had already bent Mari over the edge of the sofa and was lifting his skirt up over his ass. Yvette's eyes went wide and he shook his head. "Now what kind of a lesbian doesn't do pussy?" I teased. "Want to learn?"

Mari nodded. This was going to be good.

Near the sofa was a table with gloves and condoms and plastic wrap. I armed myself with a little of everything. Back at the sofa I pulled my Levi's off and sprawled out, plastic wrap at the ready.

Yvette learned fast, even if clit-licking through plastic was a little like going down on an inflatable doll. "It's kind of like rimming," he said.

"Sort of, except with this, you're not supposed to stop. Quit talking."

Right next to us Ariel was reddening Mari's exposed ass with methodical spanks. Mari wiggled just like Sweet Gwendoline, and I hoped the gaff was designed for hard-on control. Ariel switched rhythmically from one cheek to the other, and when she was done, red fishnet marks covered Mari's ass. The marks looked hot.

I told Yvette to put on a glove and lube it up. "Okay, now slide two fingers in my pussy, babydyke," I said to him, "real slow, under the plastic wrap. Leave the plastic over my clit and keep licking." With only a little effort he got his movements coordinated. His right hand pumped slowly in and out of my cunt while his tongue lapped over my clit.

Ariel ripped Mari's fishnets with a fast, sharp tug. The red impressions of the netting were easy to see now. I looked up and found Margy lurking a couple of sofas away, watching us all intently. Her door shift must be over. I glanced over at Ariel to see what she was up to. She'd seen Margy too.

"Call her over?" I asked. Ariel nodded, a really wicked look in her eyes.

"Margy, come fuck some sweet ass," I called, and it took the blue-eyed devil about a quarter of a second to get over to where we were. "Whose?" she said innocently, but we all knew who she'd taken a shine to. Mari's ass twitched a little. I wondered if it was involuntary or a special fag sex club come-on.

"Need to borrow a dildo?" Ariel asked. Margy shook her head and stroked her crotch – of course she was packing. Between my legs Yvette was flagging a little because he was so interested in the fix Mari was in. "Keep going!" I hissed. But in fact I was pretty interested in Mari's predicament too. "Will that gaff hide his cock and balls?" I whispered. Yvette nodded – which was great, since that movement sent me swooping up towards orgasm. He felt the change in my energy and got suddenly into it, and within two minutes I was writhing on the sofa, pulling the sheet up where it was tucked between the cushions, clutching Yvette's shoulders and gasping as I rode all the way through a very hot come. When I was done I pulled him up to cuddle next to me, and he nodded over to the scene that had developed on the other end of the sofa.

Ariel still had Mari bent over the sofa's arm, but now she was at his head. I had to concentrate a little to hear her talking to him. Margy was already in his ass with her long, substantial dick. It was silicone and not quite the right shade to be flesh tone – hers or anybody else's – but who cared? Mari, in the position to be most impressed, couldn't see it anyway. I couldn't tell, from where I sat, if the gaff was doing its job – Yvette felt me crane my neck to try to catch a glimpse of it, and whispered, "Don't worry, we've picked up straight guys and let them fuck us. They never had a clue. She won't see his cock."

That was almost as titillating as the scene before me. "Straight guys?"

"Yeah, we go to that karaoke bar down by the airport."

"God, you guys are total sick fucks!" It was hard to keep my voice to a whisper. I felt as much admiration as revulsion hearing this little secret.

"We are, aren't we?" Yvette said it with pride.

"Totally! *Karaoke!*"

Margy wiped that image out of my head when her savage grunts started. She was throwing the long dildo into Mari so hard that the little fag gripped Ariel's arms to keep his balance. Margy had his hips and wasn't just thrusting into his ass – she pulled him onto her dick, too, with each thrust. The base of the dildo must have been banging her clit something fierce. Mari began grunting too. I wondered admiringly if we were coming up on a simultaneous orgasm. Ariel talked quietly into Mari's ear, a filthy stream of gutter talk that Yvette and I heard only snatches of. You could always count on Ariel for that. "Fucking open pussyhole of an ass, take it up your slutty..." we heard. "Fuck you like the whore bitch you are, fucking..."

It was a good thing Margy could handle trash talk. I'd met some lesbians who'd run crying from the likes of what came out of Ariel's mouth when she got turned on. But Margy was the kind of butch who could roll with it, so Ariel's gutter talk only escalated the fuck. Pretty soon both of them were yelling like they were trying to cheer each other on. "Oh! Yeah, please!" Mari cried, still somehow managing to keep his voice high enough to draw no suspicion. Margy was practically roaring. Yvette rubbed his pussy through the silk panties he wore over his gaff.

I didn't come any more that night – it felt too much like chaperoning at Satan's Academy for Young Ladies, and I was still a little worried about my reputation. But by the time the boys were unmasked, about four in the morning, they'd made themselves so popular that none of the remaining hard-core girls – including Margy, who seemed positively smitten with Mari – seemed to care. In fact the only repercussion of the charade turned out to be my favorite part. Danny, the big butch punk dyke whose warehouse Clitosaurus occupied, insisted that the boys do a fuck show for the girls. Everybody sat sprawled on the sofas jilling off or doing each other while Mari yanked Yvette's leather pants down around his ankles, bent him over the railing, and butt fucked him real good. The short velvet skirt flipped around while Mari plowed his friend – too cute. Danny even pulled out a Polaroid and some of the dykes got their pictures taken with Yvette and Mari.

The next month Danny spread bar cards all over the city for her new club Queeradox, "where fags and dykes go for transgressive love!" Ariel and I were regulars. So, naturally, were Mari and Yvette, who started telling the new girls that they were sisters, even though Yvette was blond and Mari's mother was Filipina.

DEMETRIUS' STORY

It had been wild enough finding Jack, and now this – with Demetrius around, I had two daddies for the price of one. Neither man had given any indication that they intended to stop seeing each other now that Demetrius was back in town, but I also received no signals that Jack would stop running with me. One of these days, I guessed, I should initiate one of those "So what are we doing here, anyway?" conversations that I was used to having with women on the second or third date. Maybe you could take the dyke out of the U-Haul, but not the U-Haul completely out of the dyke. In the meantime the new turn of events tickled me so much that I went around humming Holly Near's "Imagine My Surprise," feeling pleasantly perverse about the whole thing.

If Holly had met the likes of Jack and Demetrius, I thought, lesbian and bisexual history might have played out a little differently.

But I was also puzzled. I'd been rejected by gay men for years, and now all of a sudden they surrounded me. Had I tapped into a secret bisexual vein of leather daddies? Were they using me as an exotic and strange experiment? (Not that I cared if they were. *Use me until you use me up*, as the disco diva implored.)

So next time we all got together, I asked them.

"I don't know about calling myself bisexual," Jack grumbled.

"I can't imagine what adjective better describes you with my dick up your ass and your dick balls-deep in Miranda's pussy, Mr. Lucky Pierre," said Demetrius. "Remember what Doctor Kinsey said – 'bisexual' ought to be used as an adjective, not a noun."

Jack and I both said we could think of an awful lot of relevant adjectives, but Demetrius's point was well taken.

"You just feel freaky about calling yourself bisexual because you're worried about what everyone will say."

"No, that's not it at all," said Jack. "I just don't see myself as resembling the men in the bisexual community."

"You resemble *me*," said Demetrius pointedly. "I've never called myself anything else. Well, since I came out."

"Yeah, don't forget, when I met you you'd just escaped from being straight."

This seemed all but inconceivable to me, since Demetrius embodied for me the queer elegance that only a big, slightly butch-of-center African-American queen could. I told him so.

"Thank you, sweetheart. I must say I did always have a bit more style than the hopeless men who surrounded me. And it's true that in the gay world I have blossomed very nicely. But yes, I came rather late to all this, compared to you and Jack."

So Demetrius told me his story.

"I GOT MARRIED soon after I graduated from high school, and my wife and I jumped into adult life with both feet. We both worked and attended night school, because we were determined to get a college education, and we couldn't afford to do it any other way. We started a family earlier than we planned to – thank god Aletha's mother could help out with the baby – and all through my twenties I worked just about as hard as it's possible for someone to work who isn't toting barges and lifting bales. Aletha and I both got degrees, and I got a good job that let her go on to law school. You've never seen a couple that wanted so hard to climb the ladder. We wanted our child to have better – and we wanted to have better ourselves.

"We always had a pretty good relationship. We loved each other and our son, and we had as good a sex life as we could manage given how busy we were with work and school and taking care of family. Of course, while we were on the fast track to the upper middle class, most of our friends from high school were growing up a little more gradually, and the rare times I saw my old crowd they all seemed to find more time for fun than I did. I didn't drink or do drugs, I didn't have time to fuck around. I was saving it all up, I guess.

"I passed over ten years living like this. Aletha got out of law school, passed the bar, and joined a firm that kept her even busier than I was. I spent as much time as I could with our son.

"But after I turned thirty I started to crack. I didn't drop a single responsibility, but I began making time for myself, and the way I did it was to begin exploring my sexuality. I had no idea who I really was underneath, see? At first it didn't even occur to me to try sex with men. To begin with, I went to peep shows and saw call girls. I made friends with a couple of them, and that's how I found the leather community. One of the women invited me to go to an S/M party. I told myself I was just going to watch, to check out these strange people and their kinks."

"Famous last words," said Jack.

"Well, naturally. Sometimes I wonder if people who don't have these sexual interests, no matter how deep they're buried, even notice the dominatrixes and leather folk and sadomasochists in their midst. But this party got my attention in such an intense way, I knew I had to start exploring the scene. I just stood there while my friend went off and played. I was riveted by one woman, a tall and deeply imperious Mistress. In retrospect I realize how masculine she was. Not butch – actually masculine, though she was also deeply female. That was her style. She had on a black men's-cut suit in a butter-soft lambskin, very Dominatrix-as-CEO. At the end of the evening I finally summoned the courage to approach her and begged to know if I might give myself to her, if there were something I might do to please her.

"Naturally, she was a pro, and she gave me her card. A clean white engraved card with her number and the words 'Georgia Strong, Consultant.'"

"Is she still around?" I asked. I had never seen anyone like her at a party, though the reverence in Demetrius' voice as he described her made me think I could use some consultation.

"No, Miranda, she left town a couple of years later. Now she keeps an office in New York, and she did have one in Hong Kong, though I don't know if she'll keep it when the Brits leave. She calls her work spaces 'offices,' not 'dungeons,' as I discovered when I called her the next day. I had asked my friend about her and she told me Georgia had a very good, if severe, reputation.

"I call her 'Georgia' now only because I am no longer submissive to her. Then, of course, I called her 'Mistress Strong,' or sometimes 'Sir.' Somehow her workplace persona suited me, as hard as I'd been working to succeed in business. And her femaleness was just present enough to keep me caught up in her maleness."

"Is that why Jack plays with me? I have enough maleness to keep him interested in my femaleness?"

"Very analytical," Jack growled. I ignored him. Demetrius seemed like a bigger expert at the moment.

"That's part of it. Of course, someone who was not at all open to bisexuality wouldn't respond that way. But there's also something very powerful about true androgyny, about mixing the characteristics so they're not sublimated in each other but still both present, with all their erotic charge. You do have that, Miranda, and Georgia had it in spades. Sometimes I would kneel in front of her and have the almost hallucinatory experience of feeling her gender switch back and forth so rapidly I could hardly keep up.

"A really skilled top goes for your potential, I think. The

more hidden, the better. Georgia saw me completely over-whelmed, practically buried, by my heterosexuality. I was more a husband, father, and family man than I was myself. I had taken on so much responsibility that I was hungry for her authority. And she decided that the way to unleash me was to show me the path not taken.

"So she always met me and used me in her masculine per-sona. I know that she had a femme side, too, but while I sub-mitted to her, I never saw it. My training was very sexual, very over-the-desk-with-my-pants-around-my-ankles. She did not feminize me at all, either through dress or through behavior. She simply turned me into a queer man. She taught me to suck her cock as she leaned back in a big leather office chair and I knelt before her. She sodomized me repeatedly – that's what she always called it, 'sodomized' – bending me over every surface in her office. She had me masturbate for her while she stroked her big, realistic dildo, making me keep my eyes fixed on it until I shot. Then she'd order me to lick the come off my hands.

"She always stayed clothed. I never saw her harness, only her cock. I never saw a glimpse of her body. And somehow by the time she finished with me, I was hungry to unbutton a shirt and find a male chest underneath. I wanted muscles, a hard stomach, a hard cock. I still loved Aletha and the feel of her under my hands, but I dreamed of men all the time. I finally begged Georgia to give me to a man.

"She gave me two sealed envelopes and sent me to an office building downtown. I gave the first to the doorman, and he made a call to announce me, directed me to an elevator, and keyed in the access code for the penthouse suite of offices. When I got to the top, a male version of Georgia waited for me. He took Georgia's letter and gestured me into a beautifully appointed private office with floor-to-ceiling glass windows on two sides. He ordered me to strip and stand by the window. With all San Francisco looking up my ass, I obeyed him. My cock had never been so hard.

"I should tell you that, although this man was white, and I had exactly zero desire to get into a racially-charged dominance and submission thing, I did not doubt for an instant that this was where I was supposed to be. Georgia, in fact, was mixed race, which put our explorations in some way on level footing. But I barely registered this man's color – only his sex. Only his sense of authority. As he left me standing there while he read Georgia's letter I prayed that she had asked him to fuck me – or that he'd decide to do that on his own."

"Tell Randy who the man was," said Jack.

"It was Sir Sebastian, whom you have met, Miranda," said Demetrius. "He kept me there all afternoon, naked in front of the window, and took me home with him at the end of the day. I was not allowed to put on my clothes, descending naked in the elevator to his car, driving with him across the Bay Bridge, entering his big house – the same one you entered blindfolded. He did not fuck me in his office. He talked to me, told me things about men together, taught me history, explained what he expected of me. My cock never went down. I hung on his every word. At his home, in his dungeon, he shackled me to the St. Andrew's cross, electrified me with his hands, took my ass. It seemed like it lasted for hours. He took me down, kissed me, and I sobbed. I wanted to stay with him. I had never felt anything like it. But I didn't want to leave Aletha and our son."

"What did you do?" I asked. "How could you possibly balance?"

"It wasn't like balancing family time with visits to whores or even to Georgia. Sir Sebastian was prepared to accept me as his boy, but he agreed that I couldn't come to him full time. By the time I moved out for good – my son was sixteen – our relationship had changed. I had grown into myself. I was no longer a boy."

"What happened with your family?"

"Oh, they're still an important part of my life. Aletha and I are dear friends, sometimes still lovers. We transitioned better than anyone else I know who's tried to do this. It was hard at first, but I think my leaving freed her up to change in ways she'd been wanting to. You know, she'd been under just as much pressure as I had, all these years of our marriage. Tommy is finishing medical school back in New York, and I try to spend part of every year there.

"There's one more important part to this story. After Sir Sebastian released me, at a gathering of men at his house, he introduced me to Jack. He actually was behaving very much like you were the time you visited Sir Sebastian's."

"Jack, are you blushing?"

"Shut up, Randy."

"It was my privilege to pick up the pieces," said Demetrius. "I took him home with me. It took him several years to leave."

DYKE DRAMA

Gradually I had begun to tell my friends at work about Jack and Demetrius, including Sue, one of the half-dozen dykes at the company. We'd gone on a couple of dates ages ago, but it didn't work out and there didn't seem to be any hard feelings. She knew Ariel too. We'd done brunch a couple of times together. As far as I was concerned, she was one of my pals.

Until one sunny day as we spent lunch hour together at Justin Herman Plaza.

"You know, you've really changed since you started hanging around with those guys," she said. "I hardly ever see you in women's spaces any more. Don't you think you'd better spend a little time wondering why everybody you spend time with these days has a penis?"

"What do you mean?" I asked, though I knew damned good and well.

"All the fags and their big-dick fag culture," hissed Sue. "Even Ariel. They've all got dicks. There's nothing but dicks in your life right now."

"Ariel has a big clit, not a penis."

"Oh, bullshit. I don't care what you call it, it's a dick. I think you're just going straight. You're sucking it, you're fucking it. It all just sounds like straight sex to me."

I hadn't actually said two words to Sue about sucking and fucking – it didn't seem appropriate on the job, for one thing.

The sucking and fucking went on in Sue's overactive imagination, obviously, as much as it did in my private life. I figured, as overheated as she was getting, that she'd probably thought about it quite a lot.

"Sue, go work for Jesse Helms. He'll explain that whatever you call what I'm doing with the fags, it's not 'straight.' Tell him about Ariel, while you're at it. I don't think he'll consider that straight, either."

"You're just in denial, Miranda."

"Sue, my sex life is weirder than anyone else's you know, and you're trying to tell me I can finally write my mother and tell her I've gone straight. Can you tell me why your concern for my sex life is any different from an over-amped Catholic priest who can't get his mind off sodomy? Who's got dicks and how close I get to them isn't really any of your business, so what's with you?"

"I just think you've got a bit of nerve calling yourself queer," Sue huffed.

"And you've got nerve, period! 'Queer' isn't a synonym for 'lesbian,' Sue, it means a lot more than that. You and your girlfriend probably have straighter sex than I do. And anyway, who the fuck cares? Besides you. There's only one thing about my relationship you can count on – you're not invited."

I left her chewing her sandwich and scowling.

ARIEL MAKES LATTES

Ariel and I hardly even bumped into each other any more. She had some new babe in her life, plus she worked constantly, and I was spending lots of time with Jack and Demetrius. We left each other notes every day – we wrote them on the same piece of paper, so by the end of the week the sheet that had been blank on Monday was filled with conversation in two distinct hand-writing styles: "Have a good Monday. Love you, hon." "You too – I won't see you tonight, I don't think – can I have the last bottle of wine in the fridge and replace later?" "Sure, doll. Stay safe." "Thanks. Always." "Babe, I might be gone for a couple days – will you be sure to feed the cats?" "Of course – tied up with the boys again? Heh heh."

So I almost jumped when I entered the kitchen and saw her in a silky lounging robe, paging through the paper. She had the little stovetop espresso machine going, the one I could never get to work right. She had a big cafe latte in the works.

"Ariel! You're home! You're awake!"

"Hi doll. I missed you, figured if I got up a little early I'd catch you before you went out to earn a new piece of your leathers. Want a latte? You're looking at me like I just stepped off the ceiling of the Sistine Chapel. I guess that's a yes."

"Damned right it is, and you *are* an angel."

"Just of the sleazy night streets," Ariel said with a sigh. "I float along a few inches above the earth, and all the johns are convinced I have a halo, except for the ones who think I'm Satan Incarnate. Of course, some of them like that about me. Myself, I think it's more like purgatory, at least on my bad nights. It's a good thing I haven't decided whether or not to get my dick surgically turned inside out, 'cause I sure as hell can't afford it yet."

"How many blowjobs laid end to end will pay for one sex change?" This was a joke I'd actually heard first from her. She said after she had this figured out that she was going to write it up as a scholarly monograph and submit it to the scientific journals that printed "all that boring bullshit the sex change doctors write."

"I know one thing, I've certainly gotten good at it. Maybe one of the nice doctors would like to consider a trade account." She fussed over the espresso gizmo, which had begun to spit dark, redolent coffee into a mug. She deftly switched mugs in mid-stream, making me one too. After the shots of espresso had burbled out, she steamed some milk in a long-handled pot and mixed it with the coffee. She handed me my mug, which had "Good girls go to heaven, bad girls go...*everywhere*!" printed on the side. Hers said "Love your hair! Hope it wins!" Ariel collected mugs like that. She was ridiculously easy to buy gifts for, because every shop in the Castro tried to outdo the next with queer mugs for the tourists to take home. The first Christmas after we broke up I got her one that said "An army of ex-lovers cannot fail!" She laughed for days.

"Maybe you should just keep the dick and use the money you save to go to law school. You can start a new mug collection then. They make great ones for lawyers."

"Well, that presupposes that I'm saving anything, but frankly, some of my post-op friends don't sound too thrilled with the functional state of their new parts, so maybe my being an attorney would actually bring more pleasure to the world."

"I think you're bringing plenty of pleasure to the world as a whore, Ariel, the question is whether you want to keep doing it forever. I know I like hearing your 'How was work today, dear?' stories better the way things are now, but if you want to go to shark school, I'll support you every inch of the way."

"Thank you, baby, and I *am* thinking hard about it. I bet I'm the only one of your friends who has to decide between getting a pussy and becoming a lawyer."

"The only one. God, you make good lattes."

"Don't get your hopes up, Randy. It's not a career-level skill. I did that before I started whoring, and if it were that pleasant or lucrative, maybe I wouldn't be sucking dick for dollars."

"Do they ever want to suck yours?"

"The customers?" Ariel laughed. "Honey, you *know* they do. There's nothing like a long tall drink of water with an eight-inch hard-on to confuse a guy. I know it bothers some of 'em that they get so turned on, but lots of those men know exactly what they want."

"Jack's always making jokes about being confused by me."

"That's because getting into you means that he's at least a little bit bisexual, and by definition confused." She saw me start to get fired up and held up her hand to stop me. "That's defined by the folks who are so stuck in their ruts that it greatly confuses them to imagine being able to get into anyone regardless of their genital geography. The guys who get into me are probably at least a little bit bisexual too – unless there's a special sexual orientation for people who like trannies. Some people say there is."

"What do you think?"

She sighed. "I'm really not sure. On the one hand, when people get hot for me because I'm a 'she male,' they're getting turned on to male and female characteristics simultaneously. That's pretty bisexual, you know? But then, some of these men would never, ever fuck a regular man. They need my tits to be there, and for me to seem female in other ways. Then they can get into my cock. Or once in a while it's vice versa. Gay men who aren't interested in pussy, but they can do it with me because I have male genitals."

"You don't usually put it that way." In fact, I'd never heard her refer to anything about herself as "male."

"You mean, when I say, 'Of course they're female genitals. They're mine'? Male-looking is what I mean, I guess. Actually, I think they *are* male to most of my johns. Getting them to think that a penis could be 'female genitals' is too much for them. Fucking me in the first place is all the gender crime they can handle."

"Gender crime?"

"Yeah, you know, people are supposed to be only one gender, not both at once. It used to be that you had to stick with the body you were born into no matter what. Now we can change, but transsexuals are still outside the pale for almost everyone. But it's not just us and our lovers who commit gender crimes. There are sex criminals, too. People who don't have sex the way they're supposed to. Everyone's supposed to be heterosexual, for instance, and you see how well that rule's being followed."

"Around here, hardly at all!"

"Well, certainly not in *our* house. See, that's a gender crime *and* a sex crime, because gays and lesbians are stepping outside of gender expectations when they have sex with someone of their own sex. 'Opposite' sex – now there's a concept. But no matter where you look, compulsory equals boring. No wonder people resist."

"So you don't think people are born queer, or trans, or whatever?"

"Well, sure I do. Some of us, anyway. But sex and gender have had all these rules made around them because people are supposed to breed and work. They're supposed to listen to authority figures and pop out the next generation and keep them in boot camp until they're old enough to have their own babies. Every generation or two we send a whole lot of them off to get killed in a war. Rebellion is inevitable. We commit gender crimes and sex crimes to differentiate ourselves from the herd of sheep who're still doing basically what the Catholic Church told their great-great-great-great-great-grandparents to do."

"Ariel, you're pontificating."

"Yeah, and on just one latte, too. It's unbelievable. Want another?"

THE MACHINE HISSED AND SPIT, and under Ariel's ministrations a fresh latte appeared. I gathered a finger full of the foam and sucked on it.

"What's up, honey? You seem all heavied out all of a sudden."

"Um, Ariel...do you think I should get a sex change?"

"What?" Ariel – who was usually completely unflappable – looked as surprised as I'd ever seen her. "Why the hell are you suddenly gender dysphoric before breakfast? Jesus, I can barely keep up with my own gender, and now you."

I felt pretty surprised myself. I hadn't even known consciously that I was going to say it, and now I was stuck trying to explain something even I didn't understand.

"I...I guess I've been thinking about it because of Jack."

"Like maybe he'd rather have a real boy than Memorex?"

"I guess." I took a long slug of my latte for fortification.

"Darlin', tell me. When you were little, did you keep waiting for your penis to grow in?"

"No."

"Did you feel trapped in the body of a girl, like it was the wrong body for you?"

"No."

"When your breasts started to grow, did they humiliate you? More than the average pubescent girl, that is."

"I don't think so."

"Well, *voilà*, then chances are you're not a true transsexual. You'd flunk the intake at the gender clinic, anyway. If you're going to go through with this, I can see I'll need to make some flash cards and work with you until you can go in there and seem genuinely gender dysphoric. Now for the next set of challenging questions. Do you like your body the way it is? As much as any American woman can be said to like her body, given that we're supposed to think we're supposed to look like anorexic fourteen-year-olds?"

"Basically, yes."

"Specifically, do you like your breasts and your cunt?"

I squirmed a little. I was thinking of the last action my breasts and cunt had seen – just a couple of nights ago. There was also the fact, of course, that my breasts and cunt had seen plenty of action with Ariel herself over the several years I'd known her. So that answer definitely had to be a "yes" too.

"Do you want a penis?"

"Sometimes, sure."

"Now we're getting somewhere. A correct answer! And I sure wish we could just trade, since I'd be more than happy to have your cunt and I'd love to know that my old penis was in good hands with you. But here's a harder question: Do you want a penis like Jack's? Or even like mine? One that gets hard and gets off, and that you feel sensation through?"

"Of course!"

"Well, that's the problem, my little man. I assume you want this cock partially because you think it would be cool to have one" – here I nodded – "and I can't deny that sometimes it is, even though I'm contemplating sacrificing mine to the great god BMW-For-My-Doctor." I giggled. "But I imagine you also want one because you think it would please Jack. Him being a man's man, and all."

I nodded. Yes, that's exactly what I thought. From the very first day, I'd wondered how long a man who loved cock would stay interested in my cunt.

"So I'm right. The jokes about confusion could stop, and you could go to the Blow Buddies with him without fear of detection. No more packing that tacky little Realistic. You could stand up to pee."

"All that, yes."

"Well, here's the bad news, bro. You won't get a dick like that. They don't make 'em at the factory. Have you ever seen a naked FTM?" I shook my head. "I suppose you think medical science gives a shit. Oh, honey, I'm so sorry. It would be a glorious gift to Jack and to yourself – at least to your Randy persona, I'm not sure Miranda will know how to accessorize it – but the cock you're fantasizing isn't available yet. Just a minute." Ariel put down her coffee and disappeared down the hall. When she came back she had a textbook. It fell open to pictures of the other surgery – male-to-female – but a few pages later she found the female-to-males. She was right. The pictures labeled "phalloplasty" and "metoidoplasty" didn't begin to match my fantasy cock.

"Look, Randy, we make do with what we can get. Many of us want the surgery no matter how underdeveloped it still is. Maybe in thirty or forty years the doctors' work will look and function great. Right now, most of us – if we're really telling the truth – will say it ain't perfect, much as we support each other's right to have the surgery done in the first place. I mean, what do you suppose the doctors would think if we all just boycotted them? If we said, 'You aren't getting a cent of our money until you can do this right?' But that won't happen, because so many of us are desperate for the surgery."

"Ariel, I must sound ridiculous to you. Like a total dilettante. And after you made me those great lattes."

"Truth serum, Randy. You have to watch out when I make you coffee. You won't be able to hide anything from me. And now that you're in my power, let me ask you why somebody as happily bisexual as you are is so tweaked about Jack being bi."

"But he's not, Ariel. I'm like an anomaly to him. I can't actually believe it's gone on this long."

"I believe he called you a 'science project,' not an 'anomaly.' And you know what I think? I think you spent too much time getting kicked out of bed by fags before you met Jack. You keep expecting the bottom to fall out. You can't accept it that he

just digs you and what you two do together. Or three, or however many you had lined up this weekend."

"But..."

"But nothing, chick. Look, in this town we pretty much
agree that each of us can identify any way she wants or needs to.
You are kind enough to call me a woman in spite of my embarrassing and unwomanly penis. I'm glad to call Jack anything he
wants to be called, including Mr. Gay San Francisco. But the
pure fact is, if Dr. Kinsey were poking around here asking questions, Jack's behavior would come out on the chart looking
bisexual. I'm sure he knows it too. It's none of our faults that the
queer community has its collective panties in a twist about
bisexuality. Remember what I said about the confusion being in
the mind of the labeler?"

I nodded.

"Well, so I think that what's really going on is that you don't
want to be a man – except the part of you that's a boy right now,
maybe. What you want is to not worry that Jack will get freaked
out about his relationship with you, have no support for it, and
bail."

I felt like crying. Ariel had nailed it.

"And what I want to counsel you to do is, stop projecting
freak-out onto him. The more you project it, the more likely he'll
be to experience it. It'll be in the air, and harder for him to avoid.
Have you even talked to him about any of this? Does he know
we're about to become the House of the Rising Transsexuals?
Are you sure he'll appreciate all the trouble you're taking to
patrol the borders of his sexual orientation for him?"

"Well, we have talked a little, but..."

"But damned little, I'll bet. Maybe I'll get him a t-shirt made
that says, 'Shut your mouth, the little fish is with me.'"

"Ariel!"

"And on the back it can say, 'Yeah, her dick comes off, but
it's bigger than yours and it never goes soft.'"

Ariel was enjoying this way too much.

CRAWLING TOWARDS THE CASTRO

It was a nice day and Jack and I had decided to walk to the Castro. Being out on the streets, or in public anywhere, with him meant dealing with the fact that men who were hell-bent on cruising him looked right through me. If he wanted to, Jack could have abandoned me behind every dumpster from SOMA to 18th and Castro, going off each time with a different hunky Latino party boy, silver-bearded fox, or goateed and slumming Greens busboy. I knew that San Francisco had once had even riper cruising, but from the looks Jack got along Market Street you'd think he had single–handedly revived the Summer of Love. This didn't do wonders for my confidence. I don't know why it was shaky; Jack showed no signs of getting tired of me. Now that Demetrius had come back, we made a sort of family, with me alternating between a few houseboy duties and Daddy's Boy status.

Still, all the contradictions that had come tumbling out during my conversation with Ariel still nagged at me. I decided the time we spent walking could do double duty as check-in time – but where to start?

"Jack...are you sure you wouldn't say you're bisexual?"

In the middle, I guess.

Jack gave a long sigh, like he'd been expecting this. "No. I don't know. Maybe." He glared at me. "No, that sounds confused – which I'm not. I have a dick. I use it."

"So you're phallocentric!"

"Randy, damn it, just ask Demetrius. He'd say I was butt-hole-centric. Why are you grilling me about my sexual orientation all of a sudden?"

"Wellll..."

"'Cause I'm hanging around with you in the first place?"

I peeped up through my hair, trying to mimic the submission gesture of an adorable puppy. I nodded.

"I was a fag, then I got my dick wet, now I must be bi? At least you didn't ask if I'd gone straight."

"Jack, don't get the wrong idea. I don't want you to go straight. If you did I'd probably run screaming. I just, you know, get nervous about what this all means, and that I don't know any role models, and..."

Jack grabbed the back of my neck and shook, gently. "Randy," he said, "you think too much."

"I can't help it."

"You want a role model, look at me and Demetrius. We've been running together for years. Sometimes we're in the same town, sometimes we're in different hemispheres. It evolves but it never changes, we don't put too many conditions on it other than caring about each other and respecting each other and being hot for each other. It works out."

"But, Jack, you're both men!"

Jack really growled now. "Randy, do you really think that makes one fucking bit of difference? Why do you think so many of our queer brothers and sisters are lining up to get hitched? Because they can't figure out how to do it without social formalities. Well, we don't have those, except for collars and keys. And we don't need 'em. A vote for gay marriage is a vote for gay divorce, and it's all bullshit as far as I'm concerned. You love somebody as long as you love them. If they love you back, that's gravy. You cherish what you have until it changes, it goes away, or you die. It's real simple. It's just that people usually think they need to live by complicated principles, not simple ones. You can give me all the air you want about how women are raised different, but I don't buy it. Sure they are, and maybe you were raised the same way, but then why can I take you into Ringgold Alley and piss on you and not have you call the cops? Most women aren't like you, you know. Some of us are just different, Randy. I'm one and you're one. Do you really need to give it a more complicated name than that?"

"Wow, Jack, I've never heard you make a speech before!" In fact, what he said made me feel much better. "But see, whenever I talk about this to my dyke friends, well, except Ariel, they go off about gender and how men do things differently and they tell me it'll either get more heterosexual or you'll get bored or..."

"Excuse me, Randy, but Daddy thinks you need some *new* dyke friends. No fucking wonder you're all up in your head!"

"See, and the other thing is, gay-maleness just seems so incompatible with...with fucking a woman. If you felt like you were bisexual, it might seem more...um..."

"Miranda, did you pick this shit up in Gay and Lesbian Studies or where? Maybe your problem is that you came out in an era when queer people spend more time theorizing than they do in the sack. Haven't I been keeping you sufficiently occupied? Instead of wondering when the next time is you'll get to lick my boots you're playing a solo game of 'What's My Sexual Orientation?' Maybe you should be *crawling* towards Castro Street."

"Jack, what you're saying is really reassuring and everything, but I just get nervous! I mean, before I came along you were practically a gold-star fag, and now...I mean...I don't even have a dick or anything!"

Jack stopped short at this. "*Penis envy?* We burned cop cars on White Night and fought a killer virus so you fucking kids could revive *penis envy?* Randy, you have about fifteen dicks. If it would make you feel better we can go over to Good Vibrations after brunch and get you another one. You've also got two hands which, when balled into fists, are just slightly larger than Demetrius's cock, though don't make a big deal out of that to *him*. The night I picked you up I expected to get yet another Queer Nation boy too scared to really fuck and too full of himself to really give it up. Instead I got something that hadn't happened for way too long – I got surprised. And I like that, and I don't give a shit what your gender or your orientation or your hat size is. You surprise Jack Prosper, you can stick around while he waits to see if you can do it again."

"How'm I managing?" I ventured.

"Well, this penis envy shit has me reeling, though I'm not sure that's what I mean when I say I like to be surprised." He started walking again and I hopped to catch up.

"Jack, I'm not envious of penises, not really. I just worry that because you eroticize them so much, you might stop eroticizing *me*, and I don't want that to happen. See, when I'm with a woman, this doesn't even cross my mind, because I figure she isn't really into cocks. I know she's going to be happy with fingers and tongues and hands and strap-ons. But you've been into cock since forever, and I just worry that I can't measure up."

"But if women who like to get fucked are happy with all those things that aren't penises, why wouldn't a man be? When you're horny and someone's doing you with a dildo, do you really wish for a cock instead?"

"No."

"So why do expect it's so different for me?"

"I guess I've run into so many guys who..."

"...who threw you out of bed. Yeah, and back in the '70s you used to have to have the right logo on your polo shirt, too. You know, you romanticize gay men so much that you've completely missed a salient fact."

"Which is?"

"That some of them are idiots. Just like everybody else. And a lot more live in an imagination-free zone, just like everybody else. And I'm telling you, we are not like that. You're not, and

I'm not. You developed your boy persona without very much positive feedback. But you developed it anyway. And most women with such a strong boy persona would have left their feminine side in the dirt. But you have a whole closet full of red dresses. Look, Randy, you're an individual. You want me to say I'm bisexual because you're a woman, okay, I'll say it. It's no skin off my ass. But I don't love women. I love *you*. Far as that goes, I don't like most men all that much either. But I'd die for the guys in my tribe. Now are you beginning to get it?"

"Um..."

"See, it's all well and good to call yourself whatever. I answer to faggot and gay male and leatherman and all those names, but if answering to a name means I can't do something I decide I want to do, fuck it. And if someone wants to give me shit for what I decide to do, it's *their* problem."

"Don't you ever get scared that the men at Sir Sebastian's will reject you? You said some of them were really old guard."

"I love and honor the Old Guard for their ways, but some rules exist just to prop up somebody's prejudice, and they're bull-shit just like any other rule that's meant to ensure conformity. My friends will either see your spunk and your willingness and your devotion to me and respect it, or they won't. If a big bad outlaw leatherman is gonna get scared by a little pussy, I'm not going to lose any sleep worrying about his tender sensibilities."

I sighed. "I wish more guys were like you."

"Well, maybe I've begun to wish more women were like *you*. Then maybe calling myself bisexual would make sense. Because believe me, if I had any objection to fucking pussy I never would have fucked yours, dear. I did not just screw you that first night to be polite. And if you had pulled the old 'your dick's been in here, now it's mine' routine, you would have been out on your pretty femme ass. You *earn* your place in my tribe." He put his hand on the back of my neck, warm, reassuring, proprietary. It echoed his word "tribe." "And make sure I earn my place in yours. Make sure every person you play with more than once is next to you for a reason. It's your skin, you don't want it rubbing up against the sweat of losers and fools."

Tentatively I put my arm around his waist, and he answered with a squeeze.

"See, queer men have made a world together because we share the same values. We didn't set out to exclude women, at least most of us didn't. But women didn't fit in. We grew up seeing women as hypocritical and manipulative. They used sex to get things, or they resisted having sex altogether when what we wanted to do was explore sex. They wanted to have families. They wanted to exert ownership over us. Now, I'm not trying to say anything against women, because I believe society trains women to act that way. But we reject it, is all. In a world where men don't have to maneuver around all that, we come up with different rules about sex and relationships.

"In fact, a lot of the men I've known who call themselves bisexual still partly buy into the other set of rules. Like, maybe they want a family. Or maybe they feel they need women in their lives partly because of propriety, to please their parents or their boss, to not stand out as gay men, or whatever. They see reasons to play the sex and relationship game that way, and if it works for them, fine. Gender differences are important, Randy, but only because so many people never question them. They just live by them. That I was surprised to find you proves it. That you're different from most women proves it."

"Some women have always been different, Jack."

"I'm sure, and lots of *them* have turned out to be lesbians. So that's two reasons I haven't thought about them as potential sex partners. What I want to know is, how did you get to be such a rebel girl?"

"I don't know, I guess I just kept following what made me hot. I've always liked fucking men, but straight men play games too, you know, really stupid ones sometimes. Being with women felt wonderful, but I still wanted men too, and then after I came out I was around more and more gay men, and I found them so sexy, and I could just enjoy them without having to put up with any of the 'Me Tarzan, you Jane' bullshit or 'You like to fuck so much, you must be a whore' bullshit. It's ironic that we can appreciate each other better when we think we're out of each other's leagues as fuck partners. That's what gay men meant to me at first. I could appreciate their maleness, yet they weren't playing stupid courtship games."

"Do you think most queers reject hetero courtship games more than they reject the other sex?"

"Probably. Plus even when they reject each other for sexual reasons, queer men and women usually do it on the basis of sex they've had when they were pretty young. If teenage sex is the standard, it's a wonder even heterosexuals grow up to be heterosexual."

"Yeah, Randy, but you make it sound like the reason we're queer has to do with nightmarish prom dates. What about same-sex desire? Surely queers have more of that."

"Well, sure we do. But we also just have less reason to repress it. So we get to revel in what straight people are busy trying to ignore."

"You're one of those 'Everyone is really bisexual' flakes, aren't you, Miranda?"

"I don't think everyone is. I think most people would be bisexual if homophobia and gender roles were wiped out."

"Oh, *that'll* happen any day now."

I hugged Jack. "Well, we managed to solve the problem of the polo shirts."

"And instead we got rainbow flags pasted on every conceivable household product. Yeah, we queers have everything all figured out."

AFTER BRUNCH HE STEERED me up the street to a leather shop.

"Where are we going now, Jack?"

"We're buying you chaps. One of these days we'll want to get you all dressed up. Anyway, that conversation was such an intensely sadomasochistic experience, I feel like commemorating it."

HE TOOK ME HOME and told me to put on my new chaps and my vest. Then he told me to suck his cock. I swallowed it – I loved that first minute when it was still soft, loved when it came erect in my mouth – and when it had gotten fully hard, he threw me back onto the bed. In a second he had me pinned and penetrated, no warning or preliminaries – not that I needed any.

As his hips started pumping he hissed, "You're living a fag's life, Miranda. You're wearing fag clothes in a fag city and a fag is fucking your cunt. And you're a woman, and it doesn't matter except it gives me more of you to fuck. Because all those labels melt away when my dick's in you. All those labels mean shit-for-nothing when you're coming. All those labels don't affect what's in my heart, or yours. Or your spirit. Because you are *yourself*. *That's* why you're here. *That's* why I'm fucking you."

I pulled him down to kiss me, fingers full of his hair, laced around his head, and pumped my hips back up at him as fiercely as he pounded me, until I screamed and went rigid and lost myself when I came. And he was right – the instant consciousness returned, it flowed in without gender, without modifiers. Live close to that space, I thought in the moment before I lost myself again – for Jack still hammered himself into me like he was trying to pound the point home – live close to that space and all the fences we build between ourselves go down, or we float above them, needing no mooring.

RANDY'S STORY

"So what's your story, Randy?" Demetrius asked a few days later. We sat together on Jack's bed after a breakfast that he had cooked and I, trying to act at least a little bit like a houseboy, had cleaned up. "How did you come to be the kind of woman who'd dress like a boy and get picked up by a fag? How did Randy spring out of Miranda? Like Athena from Zeus' forehead? No, that's not the right metaphor."

It figured that Demetrius would be the one to ask. Jack never had, even after that last conversation, and he stayed silent now. I couldn't even tell if he was paying attention. To Jack it wouldn't have mattered if I'd recently emerged from the sea on a foam-frothed shell; I lived in his world now, and no other myths counted. Demetrius and I actually had more in common, in that we had both undergone a change from one way of being to another. So I told him my story.

"I WAS BISEXUAL all along," I began. "I came out in my late teens with a high school girlfriend – Sara. The classic thing – we were best friends, spent all our time together, and loved each other completely, until right before graduation we had sex and it changed everything in our lives. We had a three-way with a boy Sara met at a party, and she and I got so into each other that he wound up leaving! We barely had any time together – well, we spent all summer looking for places to hide and make out and explore each other's bodies, we were completely caught up in each other – but it seemed like no time had passed before we had to split up for college. We stayed connected and had wild sex when we saw each other on school breaks – at Christmas we tied each other up at her house and I came so hard we almost got caught, and on spring break we went camping and I had her smell in my nose for the next week. We just never got out of the tent, except to pee.

"We both saw guys on the side, even though we were madly in love with each other. Being madly in love didn't seem like a reason to stop fucking boys, because in a way we didn't take guys that seriously, I guess. And it would have seemed threatening only if one of us had started to fuck other girls. Fucking girls, you know, was special, and fucking boys was ordinary. That's what I thought, and I never worried about her leaving me for a boy. Only a girl. And of course, that's exactly what happened. She said she was just curious to see whether it would feel different than it did with me, but then she got entangled with this new woman. By summer vacation we were all drama and very little wild sex. I decided if she could do it, I could too, and so we broke up. When I went back to college for my sophomore year, I went right to the gay/lesbian/bi student center.

"I met a few women that way, and I made a lot of new friends. Up till then I hadn't met very many gay men. Now I had lots of them in my life, and I loved it. We shopped and dished – they taught me how to bleach my hair and advised me on what kind of makeup to buy, plus they were great to talk to, and each one was cuter than the last. Once in a while I still fucked straight boys – it was pretty easy, 'cause all around me the boys were horny and wanted to get laid – but gradually I began to regret that the guys who were fuckable weren't queer, and the ones who were queer weren't fuckable. I wanted the sensibility of my gay boy pals and some hot sexual energy too, but that didn't seem possible. Maybe some of the gay boys were willing, but I didn't know the signals.

"So I dated a few women, fucked the occasional man on the side, finished school, and moved to San Francisco. I'd taken just enough computer classes to find work right away. I checked out the bisexual groups, but mostly I felt drawn to the women's clubs. If you hang out long enough to get accepted and meet people, those clubs are a way to get into a lot of different scenes. I did my first S/M play with a woman I met at Faster Pussycat. I tended to meet a girl and date her for a while, then we'd break up or drift apart. I stayed pretty monogamous. Well, most of the time, anyway. I had a couple of pretty serious relationships. But casual sex with women was okay, too, when it happened."

"I was under the impression that you gals had a terrible time arranging for casual sex."

"Not really. It's usually more of a problem keeping it casual after the first date."

"Oh, now I remember. You move in together, right?"

"Well, I *have* noticed an underlying assumption that if you can make each other come, you must be right for each other." Jack and Demetrius laughed.

"Anyway, before I met Ariel, I had one serious relationship that lasted a couple of years. I mostly went for butches, but Jacy upped the ante. She had a lot of what the dykes call 'male energy,' even when I first met her. In retrospect, that really turned me on to her. I encouraged it, actually, because I found it so erotic. Some of her girlfriends had had a hard time with it, but not me. It sort of solved the problem of wanting hot masculine sexuality in my life, and plus she was really my first top. She kept me in short skirts with no panties, bending over the hood of the car in alleys – she was that kind of lover. I met her at a dyke sex club, and she came up to me, shoved me against the wall, and whispered in my ear, 'I have a picture of you serving me and all my friends drinks – you're naked, with a shaved cunt, and any one of us can bend you over the back of a chair and do whatever we want to you at any time. You're wearing high-heeled shoes and whatever we do to you, you never spill a drop.'"

"Fresh!" said Demetrius. "I hope you went home with her."

"Of course I did, though the gentleman's club thing turned out to be a fantasy, and she was usually too busy thinking of new ways to fuck me to teach me anything about serving drinks properly. But it didn't matter. She was the hottest thing I'd ever seen, and as long as I was her girl, I got laid as much as I could ever want.

"She packed a dildo almost all the time. At first she just thought of it as a hot sex toy. Over time, though, she got more and more into it looking extremely realistic. Just about everything I know about dildos, I learned from Jacy."

"I should really send her a thank you card," murmured Jack.

"I don't know where she is now," I said. "She left town just after we broke up."

"What happened?"

"She got so into her masculinity thing that somehow I could tell she had stopped being a butch dyke – she'd gone beyond that into something else. She started binding her breasts down and dressing to pass, and the longer it went on the more important it got to be for her. She got more and more into me sucking her cock, and she stopped wanting to go to dyke places. One night she took me to a peep show and had me kneel on the bench in the little booth while I sucked off her super-realistic dildo, and then she fucked me silly while all the women clustered around to watch us. You know peep show girls love it when people come put on a show for them. But Jacy was saying things – well, she wanted to make sure they didn't know she was a woman. She really cared that they all thought she was male, and it sounds strange, but it felt different when she fucked me from that space.

"One night I asked her point blank if she ever thought about gender reassignment, and she said yes. She'd been hanging out in the dyke community because it felt like the best place for her, but as she got more in touch with feeling male that didn't seem so right anymore. She really needed the transgender community. She needed to learn more about her options. She got more and more into her male side with support from only me, and it wasn't enough.

"The thing was, as she got more comfortable with the idea of going through gender transition, her ideas about relationships started to change. She kinda got more conservative, you know? As a man, she got more straight. Before, my submissiveness mostly had to do with sex. It just meant she wanted to fuck me all the time, and I loved that. But gradually Jacy wanted me to practically be a servant. She – he – didn't cook any more. He also got jealous of me, whereas before he'd encouraged me to do whatever I wanted. I knew he loved me, but our whole relationship just got more and more tense. You know, I didn't become queer to live a straighter life than my mother. That's what we broke up over, and then he split."

"So what about that experience turned Miranda into Randy?"

"After Jacy left, it just seemed like it was time to take stock. It took us, like, a year to break up – it was a really hard, really intense time. And after a hard breakup is a good time to look at your life in a fresh way.

"I guess I had reason to think about what really attracted me, which is some maleness and some femaleness, or at least some queerness, all mixed together. I also felt leery of getting into another intense relationship with a woman right then, although it turned out that only a few months later I met Ariel, and we were lovers for quite a while. And I liked fucking men – just not straight ones."

"Why didn't you go hunting for bi guys?"

"It's funny – by that time I'd been in San Francisco for a while, and I really wanted leathermen. And when I'd go to bisexual events, I didn't usually find that the men there had that certain something that fags, especially leatherfags, have. I couldn't even tell you what it is, but I definitely notice when a guy doesn't have it. Most bi men's style just...well, it's just different. Except yours, Demetrius, and I didn't run into you at any of those Bi-Friendly meetings."

"No, dear, I skipped those. I was too busy being sodomized. Making up for lost time."

"So you became Randy because of that?" Jack asked. I'd finally interested him in asking about the years before I rose on my half-shell! Score one for Demetrius.

"Something about hanging with Jacy while she started to go from seemingly female to male did it, I think, plus getting clear about how hot I was for gay men. After Jacy left I went to a couple of meetings for FTMs and their friends, just trying to get some perspective. One of the people there identified as a woman, but she cross dressed almost all the time. It turned me on to the idea that I could do that. Plus when I started spending time with Ariel, I met lots more transgendered people. Doing it – cross dressing, I mean, and passing as a boy – didn't seem so far-fetched then. Ariel even helped me work out my makeup. She found it too amusing for words – she just wouldn't go out in public with me when I dressed, because she said she didn't want anyone to mistake us for straight!"

"A far cry from Jacy."

"Yeah, and a big relief, too. At first I'd just dress and go where I knew fags would be. I hung out in the Castro and watched, worked on my stance, learned how to cruise. I watched young gay men, because I knew I read really young when I dressed like a boy. Eventually I could do it without getting clocked. I would sometimes make it into the bars, though often they thought I looked *too* young. I didn't have any male ID, so when they carded me I'd just slink away. Then I started to do the park. My first success was hanging out at the Midnight Sun and cruising a guy in there – when he walked out, I followed him, and he led me up to Collingwood Park, to the darkest corner. He put his hand on my shoulder – just the first hint of pressure and I was on my knees in front of him, fumbling with the buttons on his Levi's. There in the bushes I got his cock out, and the feel of it on my lips as I opened my mouth to take him sent me into a big, shivering come. He must have thought I was a nervous kid or something. Anyway, I did it – sucked him off, then managed to get out of there gracefully. If he'd wanted to reciprocate, I'd have been busted."

"That must have been a rush," said Demetrius.

"I masturbated insanely for about four days. Then I dressed and went out and did it again."

"So you got good at that – how did you deal with it the first time you got found out?" asked Jack.

"I just felt really flustered. I stammered and apologized and got out of there. That was mostly how it was, until I met you. When I found men who just wanted to get sucked, I had it easier. If a guy didn't want to get into my pants in the first place, I was home free. If all I'd wanted was to suck dick, I could have looked for the straight guys in the parks. But I wanted gay men, and mostly they wanted to do me after I did them, and that's where the trouble was."

"I can just see you out there in the park, saving dysfunctional heterosexual marriages like a cross dressed Mother Teresa," said Jack. "You know, if these boys are so straight, how do they find the park in the first place? Tearooms everywhere are lousy with them."

"I probably could have sucked dick in the alley behind Lord Jim's – or any other fern bar in the city," I said. "The point was, I didn't want straight cock."

"I know," said Demetrius, poker-faced. "It tastes completely different."

"Well, it does! On a metaphysical level, at least."

"More so to you, I think," said Jack. "To us it's just another dick in the park."

"Anyway, before you, Jack, there were a few guys who didn't freak out, but they really needed me to keep up the boy thing. No switching to femme once the scene was under way. I tried running an ad but got no answers. I didn't do it all that much when I was lovers with Ariel. But after we stopped being lovers, I really felt like I needed it."

"So that's when you found out about the dick check at Blow Buddies?"

"I found out about a lot of things that keep the girls from playing with the boys."

"I'm curious, Miranda," said Demetrius. "Wasn't all that hard on your ego? Didn't it hurt to be rejected over and over?"

"Well, sure. But the successes were so hot, they sort of canceled out the failures. Plus, I still had a femme life in the girl bars, and there I felt sexy and desired. I got enough of what I needed. Anyway, I had a very rich jerk-off life. One smoldering look from a hot daddy across a crowded room would send me home to masturbate like there was no tomorrow – and there was always Mr. Benson to fill in the gaps. I got by."

Demetrius had begun to whistle "Til There Was You."

"Then I grabbed the brass ring and found Jack, and before I knew it, you joined the family. Well, you were already part of the family, so really I joined *you*. And everything before that was just practice."

THEY REALLY DID TAKE me to Blow Buddies later that week, and Demetrius somehow managed to charm the guy at the desk into letting us in. Maybe it was the fact that he plunked his dick on the counter before even going for his wallet. He had enough dick for any three guys, and maybe the doorman figured we'd made quota.

Good thing I didn't get frisked, too, because under my boy drag I wore my frilliest lingerie – on orders from Demetrius. He didn't do domination with me on as regular a basis as Jack did, but when he said "Jump," I jumped high. The three of us crowded into one of the little cock-sucking booths that made up a maze in the back of the building, and in the dim light, with manfuck noises on all sides, Demetrius told me to strip down to my brassiere, garter belt, and fishnets. Jack stood on a bench – men usually knelt in here, because each booth had at least two glory holes – which put his cock just at mouth level. Demetrius told me to suck Jack, then took his own cock out and fucked it in and out between my held-together thighs, nudging my clit once in a while, stroking me all over and fussing with the lingerie. That way he could lean over my back and watch Jack's cock slide in and out of my mouth, and he could also talk low in my ear, too low for the men in the adjacent booths to hear.

"Babygirl, it gets even more complicated than your admittedly beautifully complicated scene, see? Here you are in your high fuck-me femme drag and you're sucking faggot dick in what might as well be a bathhouse. And fags are all around you, and you are the only fucking pussy, baby, in this whole place. Is that what you like about this, being the only cunt here, a fag goddess, a pussy in a sea of prick?"

Jack didn't have to stay quiet; he was where he belonged. His growls and moans could surely be heard all around us.

"Got my big dick slipping up against your cunt, girl. Got your throat on Jack's meat, so deep you can't go anywhere. I should fuck your cunt right now. I should tie you to a horse in the dungeon and tell all the men in this place we have pussy for them to try, if they want it. Pretty boygirl in your silky drag. If the man in the next stall looks through the glory hole he'll see your cunt all full of my meat, he'll know what you are."

Demetrius probably had no intention of sinking his meat into me, at least until we got home, since there was a no fucking rule in effect at Blow Buddies. He knew which rules to break and which to observe. But especially since my gang bang at Sir Sebastian's, the idea of being tied down and ravaged by an endless line of fags was my hottest dream, and the mere suggestion that he might preside over such a party filled my cunt with fire. My turn-on communicated itself to Jack's dick, still sliding into my throat and out. His growling lowered an octave and increased in volume. He'd shoot soon. And Demetrius now slapped his cock up against my clit, over and over – which meant I'd come soon, too.

Demetrius didn't come until we got back home. In the meantime I'd sucked a dozen strange dicks through the glory hole, having the weirdest and most wonderful reunion of my femme and fag sides I'd had since that first night with Jack. It felt like starring in a porno movie, only...queerer, much queerer.

Back home he took his cock out and worked it while Jack took over as if they'd choreographed the whole thing – and perhaps they had.

CLUB CREAM

"Tell me more about Jacy," Jack said one day. "What was the hottest time you ever had with Jacy?"

So I told him.

JACY AND I had been keeping company for several months. She was exactly the kind of woman I'd come to San Francisco to meet – tall and rangy, with a white blonde crewcut, a union job, and an arrogant streak that soaked my panties whenever she aimed it at me. At home she kept me in high heels and not much else, and she didn't bother to close the drapes. I'd never been submissive to anyone before, except once or twice, and every day when I left work I'd be so turned on to the thought of going home to her that I'd practically come whenever the bus hit a bump.

Every day it was like this: She'd hear my key in the lock, and when the door swung open, she'd be the first thing I'd see. My clothes would come off right in the foyer. She'd have the shoes there, ready for me to slip into. As soon as my feet arched up into them, everything changed. She could have me any way she wanted me for the rest of the night.

When we went out I had to be a little more dressed, of course – but usually not much. She loved me in short skirts, tight, clingy clothes, heels, lots of makeup. Women we socialized with often assumed I was a stripper. I literally never went out with her in the evening dressed in casual clothes. She always dressed in blue jeans, worn pretty tight, white shirt, black leather vest, engineer boots, leather jacket. Somehow the outfit looked right no matter where we were, maybe because she felt hot in it.

Jacy had me exactly where she wanted me, which was so turned on that I would do anything, anywhere, for her. At home I spread my legs at the slightest hint. Out driving, I flashed whomever she told me to flash. It's an absolute miracle we never got followed by a good ol' boy wanting some pussy, but we never did. I guess even to passing truckers the dynamics of our relationship were perfectly clear.

In public we were always looking for a new place to fuck. I took her fingers under restaurant tablecloths, sucked her dick in alleys, came noiselessly in movie theaters. One night in summer, a rare warm one, she took me to the top of Twin Peaks. Twenty yards away from a carload of high school students getting drunk, she told me to bend over the stone observation fence. It was just waist-high, and the rough rocks pressed into my skin. She yanked my skirt up, exposing my ass to the night breeze and anyone else near enough to see. Next I heard her spit, and a second later her cock was in me, she had me by the waist, and the whole glittering city lay below me while I held on for dear life. She was a crazy wild fuck, Jacy – she grunted and swore and called me a slutty, show-offy cunt while I clung to the stone and tried to brace my legs apart to take her.

But that wasn't even the wildest. She did scenes like that with me every week or two.

One night – after she'd had me serve her dinner naked, then made me wait, bent spread-legged over a footstool next to her while she ate it – she told me to get dressed up extra special, because we were going to a new dyke club. I was a little sullen because she hadn't fucked me, just told me when dinner was over to get up.

"Which club?" I asked as I picked out my lingerie.

"Called Club Cream. I dunno much about it. Here, wear this." Jacy pointed to a floor-length, slinky, sheer fishnet dress.

"Baby, I'd have to wear panties under that!"

"I don't think you'll need panties at this place." I glared at her and she said, "Seriously. But I'll take some along for you if you insist." And she pulled a black thong out of my lingerie drawer and shoved it into her back left pocket. "Know what this means according to the hanky code? I'm a top and I get girls to give me their underwear."

Jacy had gotten me a fine leather trench coat for my birthday, so the fact that you could see right through my dress wasn't apparent when we hit the street to hail a cab. We pulled up at a SOMA adddress I knew vaguely, though I'd never been there. "Jacy, this isn't a girl bar, is it?"

"The girls are taking over," she assured me.

Sure enough, instead of a rave, it was pretty much wall-to-wall girls. "I like women's bars best when they take over straight clubs," Jacy said. "I kinda feel like I'm trespassing."

"I like women's bars best when they're huge," I replied. "They feel so different from college-town bars that have only thirty women at any one time."

A woman sitting in front of us joined in: "Yeah, including four carloads of dykes from the next town over. I remember bars like that. But you're a city girl now. We expect three hundred women tonight at least. Can I see some ID, please? Oh, hi, Jacy."

"Hey, Bella. What's up?"

What a babe. Her chestnut curls passed her shoulders in the kind of tangle you want to dig your fists into. Her red mouth curved into a smile when she saw me scrutinizing her. I flashed her my license and she took the time to read the name.

"Hi, Miranda. My name's Bella. Have fun tonight."

"She's with me, isn't she? And we're here with our three hundred best friends," said Jacy.

"I'm having a great time already," I said, deciding that this would be a perfect time to drop the trench coat. Damn, just when I least expect it, a femme attack! And as I turned away, Jacy's hand already on my ass, I saw Bella's perfect lips curve into an even bigger smile. Over my shoulder, knowing she had a view of my ass with the hand on it, I smiled back.

"Bella's taken," said Jacy as we edged through the sea of women towards the bar. "But I bet you'd like her girlfriend, too. Mack. I should send you over there next weekend to be their sex slave, that'd earn me big points with Mack."

At the heart of the club we found the bar, teeming with women and hard to get close to – but Jacy had a way with crowded bars. She turned on the authority and got served before a long line of more patient customers. While she got us drinks, I watched the dancers – six women on high stages, one on either end of the room. Jacy came back and handed me champagne, following my gaze to the dancers' stage in front of us.

"Mack. Wouldn't you know. She probably started this club just so she could be a big ol' exhibitionist." Her free hand caressed my ass again. "Like her, baby?"

"Sometimes you run into couples and just know it'd be worth a million bucks to watch them fuck. I hope they say that about us."

"I'm sure they do."

I liked her, all right. A big, solid, copper-colored woman with eyes like a feral cat's. She danced with as much power as grace, and the way she moved her body said, "You want to feel my hands on you." I could just imagine her hands on Bella (whom I had started to think about touching, myself) – it made me shiver. Jacy felt it and her hand squeezed my ass, hard.

"Dance with me, 'Randa." Jacy pulled me into the writhing mass of dancers. She kept pulling me until we were right in front of Mack's stage. I saw Mack grin at Jacy when we got close enough for her to see us.

"Dance for her, baby. Show her something." Jacy's voice in my ear made me wet no matter what she said. "Come on, get her to look at you. I feel like showing you off once in a while."

So with Jacy at my back I turned to face Mack, and gradually I let the thumping, rhythmic beat get all the way into me, moving me like a lover moves me when we're fucking and all the way connected. Jacy was right behind me, stroking against me, hands on my hips. Mack saw, narrowed her eyes while she figured out what she wanted to do with this so-obvious come-on, then grinned again and danced right back at me. I felt like they both had cocks in me and I couldn't do anything but rock on them, let them fuck me deeper. Jacy had never pulled anything like this before, but it didn't matter.

"Don't forget, baby, she can see every inch of you through that dress," Jacy whispered. "You might as well be dancing naked. You're showing her everything right now. The only thing she can't see about you is how tight your pussy is." Her hands moved around to the front of my body now, caressing, but mostly showing me off to Mack – stroking my pussy, offering my breasts. Mack's hips made undeniable fucking motions.

"Inch the dress up," Jacy said next. "Pull it up slowly. I want your cunt, baby, now."

As I obeyed her, she rewarded me with a cunt full of fingers, entering me from behind and keeping control of my movement with one hand on my hip, pulling me into her and letting me loose so I fucked myself onto her again and again. And Mack had me by the eyes, a clear, predatory gaze that wouldn't let go. "If she wasn't up on that stage," hissed Jacy, "she'd be all over you, bitch, her fingers in your ass and her teeth on your throat. I'd let her mark you up, you wouldn't believe what she could do to you."

Jacy's fingers fucked me relentlessly, but she stopped every time I was about to come.

I sobbed with frustration when she pulled her fingers out and dragged me off the dance floor. I wasn't ready for the fantasy to be interrupted – Mack marking me up, taking my ass – but maybe now Jacy would take me someplace and really do me. Sure enough, she steered me to the restrooms, which were cavernous – we got a stall right away. She shoved me up against the wall and kissed me breathless, but instead of fucking me, she said, "You're gonna wait right here for me, 'Randa. Don't you fuckin' leave this stall." And she was gone.

I slumped onto the seat, so confused and horny and frustrated I thought I would cry. The porcelain, chilly enough to make me jump, felt good against my sweaty ass. Well, she hadn't said a word about touching myself; I felt sneaky doing it, but I couldn't help stroking my clit. It felt hot and swollen, and I wanted Jacy to get back and do something – anything – to get me off the edge. I kept stroking, feeling more defiant by the minute. Fuck her, for leaving me like this.

I climbed high, jerking myself off there on the toilet. I was just at the trembling edge of a come when Jacy came back. The stall door burst open. "Slut!" she cried, when she saw what I was doing. "I can't leave you for a fucking second!"

It took me a moment to realize that the hands grabbing my wrists and pulling me up weren't Jacy's. She'd come back with Mack and Bella, and they were the ones who held me against the wall and, almost as soon as they had me up, started to work me over. Jacy stood leaning on the stall's door frame, grinning.

"She really had her eye on your woman, Mack," said Jacy. "I'd say she wants pussy. If Bella's up for that, let's say you can do anything to Miranda you want."

Bella took my place on the toilet, skirt pulled up over her hips, and cocked her legs out at an impossible angle. She smiled sweetly, a randy come on with a sugar coating. I wanted to bite her full lips and not stop there – I hadn't seen how lush and curvy she was while she sat at the table, but I saw it now and I wanted to eat her up. But she knew where to get me started. "Miranda, baby, eat my pussy," she said, with a voice that had just a hint of "please, please, Daddy" in it, and I realized I wanted to do that more than anything.

Her cunt felt like slippery wet velvet. I knelt on the stall floor to get to her, wrapped my arms around her, ran the flat of my tongue between her lips to get her taste and felt her hard clit press back at me. I felt for the throb it gave when the blood rushed in, the little jump that lets you know she's with you.

"Her ass looks pretty fuckable, Mack," Jacy said behind me. "What are you gonna do about that?"

"Got lube with you?" said Mack.

"Of course! I don't leave home without it. I find myself wantin' to fuck Miranda at the damnedest times. Got gloves, too." The little slurp of the lube bottle opening told me something was coming, but I didn't care what. I had found a move that made my tongue very happy and that made Bella pump her hips wildly, and I had no intention of stopping until she came.

Mack's long, slim fingers, slick with lube, found my clit. The fingers of her other hand pushed into my ass. My climb toward orgasm started that instant, and Mack didn't stop – just muttered behind me about about my hot ass and Bella's hot cunt and fuckin' me and makin' me and...

In a three-way like that I'm never sure if I come as fast, distracted by what I'm doing, or faster, extra-aroused by it, because I lose track of time. Jacy managed to get in a slap on my ass once in a while. She said, "A crowd's gatherin', 'Randa, put on a good show," and that jacked me up another notch – but really all my consciousness was on Bella's clit. I didn't come until she did, with a high-pitched, breathy sob that was so sexy it just sent me over. I finally looked back over my shoulder at Mack and at Jacy.

They were both grinning.

"I'd still give a million bucks to see you two fuck," I said as we stood cleaning up at the sinks, our little crowd of voyeurs at a respectful distance.

"SO THEY TOOK US home with them," I told Jack – a little shakily, because he was fucking me pretty hard by now – "and we took turns putting on sex shows for each other until four in the morning. I even got to pull beautiful Bella's long, thick hair; I was amazed at the look in her eyes when I did. Yeah, I know I'm usually a bottom, but I wouldn't trade that memory for anything."

DRESS-UP

"You know, it's been weeks since I've seen you dress like a girl," Jack said. "I kinda miss it."

"You do?"

"Yeah, I do. There's something so – I dunno, yin/yang about a weekend when you're Randy one day and Miranda the next. Let's have a party."

"A party? Who's invited?"

"Oh, let's make it intimate. I imagine Demetrius might want to be there. Ariel? Can we have it at your house?"

"Sure, probably. Why Ariel?"

"Well, ever since you told me that story about her at the dyke club, I've been hatching this plot. I have an idea for a guest of honor, see."

"Who, Jack?"

"You'll see, baby girl."

I WAS HOME when Jack called Ariel to run the idea past her. She burst into laughter on the phone. After a conversation that last-ed several minutes, the side I could hear giving me no clues about the guest of honor – or his or her shoe size, which was part of the discussion – she hung up. She started laughing again when she saw the look on my face.

"Don't worry, baby, this isn't a set-up. It actually sounds like a delightful way to spend an evening."

And that was all I could get out of the smug bitch.

I SUPPOSE I SHOULD have felt threatened at the idea of Jack coming over to play with Ariel – the penis factor again – but except for her johns, Ariel was pretty much a dyke, and besides, the conversations I'd had with her and Jack really had been reassuring. The Saturday of our little *soirée* dawned. I spent the morning cleaning house. Ariel bustled in and out. She went to the store and got champagne and some other party food – we lived in Tenderloin Heights, close enough to Russian Hill that there were some fancy food markets within walking distance. I ducked into the kitchen while she was setting up a tray with pita and hummous.

"Don't you, like, almost always work on Saturday nights?" I asked.

"Yes." She anticipated what I was going to say next. "Some things are just worth losing money for, girlfriend. So I get my dick turned inside out a week later than I'd scheduled. Anyway, maybe I'll slip out and do a late shift. Depends how things are going."

I called Jack in the afternoon. "Daddy, what do you want me to wear? Are we talking all femmed out tonight?"

"*All* femmed out, darling. We'll need you to inspire our novice."

What*ever*! When Jack got mysterious there was nothing to do but fasten the seatbelts. Around seven it turned out that Ariel planned to get very dolled up too. This was fun. It reminded me of when we were lovers and went to the opera specifically so we could sneak into nooks and crannies and do silent, breathless little stealth fucks.

"I'll Jello-wrestle you for the bathroom," I teased.

"Forget it, I'd win. I've been Jello-wrestling since you were in junior high. I'm a champion."

"Bitch!" But a minute later she'd scooted into the living room and put "We Are the Champions" on the stereo, Freddie Mercurying me into submission. So I let her do her makeup while I picked out my clothes. I was rummaging around in my closet when I heard Ariel call, "Wear latex. You just never know when you'll wind up in the tub being pissed on by a bunch of queens."

Well, she had a point, and she knew more about the guest list and other plans than I did. I pulled out a burgundy-colored rubber tank dress and accessorized it with black opera-length gloves (I had actually worn these to the opera with Ariel, and they'd come in very handy for buttfucking while we watched "Salomé"). A pair of spike-heeled Victorian boots in a very non-retro shiny black PVC completed the outfit. I ducked in past Ariel's elaborate makeup ritual to shower.

Ariel had to powder me and we both had to yank and tug to get the dress on. "Latex is great, but it's not very user-friendly," I complained after the third time we pulled a pubic hair, but she said, "Yeah, but remember, it hoses off. Try that with silk."

We finally got it pulled down and she shined me up. I preened under her hands.

"It's been a while, Miss Thing."

"Too long, darlin'."

After I was all shiny she said, "Is there a reason almost all your femme clothes are red? Do you have a Rajneeshi past you're hiding from me?"

"No, it's just a favorite-color thing. Most of Randy's clothes are black, so I guess it helps me differentiate."

A buzz interrupted us – it was Jack at the door, with flow-ers, yet! "Jack," sighed Ariel, taking them, "if I hadn't heard all the stories, I'd think you were a gentleman."

"One has to be able to combine skills and abilities from various walks of life these days, Miss Ariel. Don't you find?"

Ariel snorted. "No shit." She headed for the kitchen to get a vase and Jack turned his attention to me.

"Hello, Pretty."

"Hi Jack." I was suddenly a little shy. "So do I finally get let in on the secret?"

"Demetrius should be here within the half-hour," Jack said. "All will be revealed."

Ariel stuck her head around the kitchen door. "Miranda, I know you're not any sort of boy this evening, but don't you think you should ask the, ah, *gentleman* if he'd like some champagne?"

Uh oh. Put a dress on me these days and I just forget how to bottom. Isn't it funny how these little things confound gender roles? Actually, that's probably a good sign. I raised my eyebrows in Jack's direction and he said, "Why, yes, I'd love some." But Ariel was already there with a flute. Playing with fags wasn't something she ordinarily did, but it was second nature to her – she'd told me long ago about how she came out as a gay man and couldn't understand why cross dressing made her happier than sucking dick.

"Was that your first clue?" I asked.

"Hardly. But in those days, in that place, when boys were feminine we just assumed they were gay. Imagine the revelation, given that I thought I was a queer boy, the first time I found myself face to face with pussy."

Ariel had poured both of us champagne too, and we sipped it and chatted about nothing much while the tension built. Jack loved this part, and if the truth were told, so did I, especially now that the party had begun and we just had to wait to see what would happen next. Before long the buzzer rang again, and Ariel said, "Miranda, why don't you get that?" But I had already jumped to my feet.

Demetrius stood at the door, as expected. Who accompanied him I didn't know, except I was pretty sure it was a young man, gracefully slender, a little taller than me, his face covered by a black leather hood. "Good evening, Miranda!" Demetrius looked like the cat who'd eaten the canary. He leaned forward to kiss each of my cheeks while the boy stood silently by. I ushered them in. Demetrius had the boy on a short leash, and he used it deftly – it looked, too, as if the boy had been leashed this way before. He moved in anticipation of the bigger man's will, and the whole scene was very smooth.

Watching the younger man move, I had the feeling that I knew him from somewhere – Blow Buddies, maybe? I knew it when Jack said, "Miranda, you asked me for something special a few months ago that I've managed to get for you – just on loan, though. Want to open your present?" Demetrius turned the boy smoothly around and unclipped his leash. He stood very silently, waiting. His hood locked at the collar, and Demetrius offered me the key.

As I pulled the hood off, my first glimpse of the person beneath it was enough to tell me who had come to visit. Before I saw his face I saw his honey-colored curls.

"*Peaches!*" Now I was all excited.

"Hi, Miranda," Peaches said shyly.

"I am in *heaven*," said Ariel. "Sweet mother Mary, that is your *real hair!*"

I looked at Jack and Demetrius quizzically. "How on earth did you score Peaches on a Saturday night? Isn't Sir Sebastian entertaining?"

"He is," said Jack, "in London."

"He doesn't travel with his retinue," said Demetrius. "I've had the pleasure of playing in his London dungeon – very nicely tricked out; you know Londoners have had so much more time to do dungeons than we have here – and he has his own staff over there. A lovely boy. Mite butcher than Peaches, granted."

"So it turns out that Peaches is quite the free lad when the cat's away," said Jack. "When we told him we could offer him a more memorable night than he could get dancing at The Stud, he was right on it."

"He has a non-Old Guard streak a mile wide, it turns out," said Demetrius. "He'll fit right in around here. But he's never done drag before."

Ariel's eyes gleamed. Jack looked at her. "Well? You're the top tonight, my dear. At least until we get this lovely boy looking a little more resplendent."

Ariel told Peaches to strip down and he did, right away. The beautiful cock I'd only seen hidden in his leather jockstrap stirred as he neatly folded his clothes. He stood before us looking perfectly composed, especially given that he was naked in a stranger's front room. I figured even if he didn't put out any more than that tonight, he'd earned a glass of champagne. I dashed to the kitchen to get glasses for him and Demetrius. I handed them over with a flourish. "Thank you, baby," Demetrius said – but Peaches winked at me!

Ariel had in the meantime been happily surveying Peaches, walking all the way around him. I knew she was calculating sizes, mentally doing his colors, planning whether to use liquid or pencil eyeliner.

"Ever been shaved, sweetheart?" she asked. Peaches nodded. "Is your ingrown problem manageable?"

"Yes."

"Oh, good. Let's all march into the bathroom then."

Ariel had picked up a big bag of disposable razors and a not-too-manly shaving cream. "Before my electrolysis," she said, "I had to get really good at shaving close. So I'll do your face. Miranda, you start on his legs. Jack, want his balls?"

"Do I ever," said Jack.

Demetrius just put the toilet seat down and sat there, arms crossed, with a big grin. "Next time," he said, "*I* want to get dressed up."

"Anything to get somebody else to shave your balls for you," said Jack.

Peaches, wetted and slicked down with the shaving cream, glowed. His cock got fatter with every long swipe of my razor – no question, because I was right in the tub with him. Jack carefully scraped his balls and pubic hair off. Ariel had his chin in her hand as she shaved his face – of the three of us, I thought, she had the most intimate job. She cooed and looked into his eyes, and I grinned – even Ariel was under Peaches' spell, and besides, the more genderfucky a scene, the less she cared about her partner's actual gender.

With Peaches' body and facial hair gone, Ariel turned the shower on and the boy rinsed off the foam. He looked sleek and somehow even more slender, and his cock – which had filled to almost full erection – looked even bigger than I'd thought it would be.

"Gonna gaff that?" asked Demetrius.

"I hope not," I said. If we gaffed Peaches, his cock would be pretty much out of reach. That wasn't what I had in mind at all.

"I think maybe Miranda's hoping to get rid of the erection through more natural methods," said Jack. Ariel grinned wickedly.

"There'll always be time for that later," she said.

ARIEL'S ROOM, just across the hall from the bathroom, had been readied for the evening's wardrobe-oriented festivities. She had lingerie laid out on the bed, and her closet was open to reveal a rack of dresses. Half her dresser was piled high with shoeboxes, the other half with her makeup kit. Two of the kitchen chairs sat in front of the dresser, a makeshift makeup station.

"Pick out a garter belt, baby," said Ariel. Peaches sifted through the drifts of sheer or lacy undergarments until he found a garter belt he liked, Ariel's second favorite one, a solid black lace '50s number.

"Oh, very utilitarian," said Ariel. "See, it has metal garters. But elegant in spite of its camp factor. I like your taste." She fastened it around Peaches' waist and then picked out matching stockings. "Cuban heel, since you're obviously not afraid of a little ostentation."

We stood watching Peaches pull the silk stockings up his newly silky legs. Ariel helped keep the seam straight and made sure there were no wrinkles by stroking her hands up the boy's shapely calves and thighs. Where the stocking ended and his shaved-smooth flesh began she stroked a little more, then fastened his garters for him. "Miranda, can you find me the black sheer mesh g-string?" she called over her shoulder, and I searched the piles of lingerie piled on the bed in search of panties while Ariel began showing Peaches pairs of shoes.

"You could just pick some," Jack suggested mildly.

"Yeah, but I want to see what his taste is," said Ariel. "That way, even if I take over, I can do a better job dressing him up in a way that makes him feel hot."

"And we thought we were accomplished tops, Jack," said Demetrius. "Then Ariel goes and unlocks the door to a whole new plane of existence."

"Yeah, well, I've spent most of the last decade on that plane," Ariel responded. "Which, in dog years, is my whole life." While she talked she methodically opened shoeboxes and offered them up for Peaches' inspection. Nothing lower than four inches, a few substantially higher than that. Ariel did wear flats sometimes, but never for dress up.

"Um, I like these the best," said Peaches finally, after having surveyed everything from thigh-high boots to sequinned silver pumps.

"Oh, *very* good," said Ariel approvingly. Peaches had pointed to a pair of black patent ankle-strap sandals with high square heels and a modest one-inch platform. "Very chic, Peaches. Shit, we should have painted your toenails, but I don't want to take the time now." Maybe only I noticed Peaches' tiny pout at this news. But he brightened up when the shoes and the g-string went on. His legs went from shapely to flawless.

"I'm really beginning to want this experience myself,"

mused Demetrius. "Ariel, can you make me look like Sylvester?"

Ariel snorted. "No doubt! And who do you want to be, Jack?"

"How about Joan Crawford?"

"Fags!" sighed Ariel. "I can feel a 'Mommie Dearest' joke coming on – or maybe a whole scene – and doubtless at Miranda's expense. Peaches, any special requests?"

"I want you to make me look like myself," said Peaches. He got a little round of applause for being so high-minded.

"For that," said Ariel, "you get to stand up and play runway model for us. Then come back to this chair for makeup." Peaches even sashayed a bit, drawing a wolf whistle from Demetrius. All the way around the bed – at the window the neon outside washed his chest and face with color, rhythmic as a heartbeat. He came back to rest at the chair opposite Ariel's, and she got to work on his face.

Peaches had a beautiful face even without makeup. With the planes of his cheekbones and the curves of his eyelids and lips accentuated with color and shadow, he looked stunning. Ariel worked fast and with complete focus. When she had almost finished she said, "Why don't you three start looking for dresses?"

Jack and Demetrius didn't need to be told a second time. They looked like they'd been waiting all their lives to rummage around in Ariel's closet. I knew what Ariel had, so I let the boys at it first. After a few minutes I heard Jack mutter, "You need tits to wear most of this stuff."

"We *have* tits," said Ariel, powdering Peaches's face. "I had to do something while I waited for the estrogen to kick in. Peaches, want to try them?"

"Sure," said Peaches. So Ariel pulled open a bureau drawer and emerged with a brassiere with built-in breast forms. Peaches held out his arms so she could fit it to his torso. Though he was a little slimmer than Ariel, the bra fit. "Oh, I just want to grab your tits now," said Ariel. But Peaches had grabbed them already.

The dress Jack and Demetrius had pulled out of the closet clung to Peaches like a second skin, accentuating the newly curvy breasts and the more angular planes of his hips and ass. It only flared out a little at the bottom of the short and otherwise clingy skirt. It was black, a slinky, stretchy knit. It had long sleeves and a bit of lace at the neck, like a coy afterthought. Peaches looked ravishing. He spun around to make the little flip of skirt swing away from his body.

"I like it," said Ariel. "There's definitely hope for you two butch numbers."

"Pretty, pretty, pretty," said Demetrius. Peaches glowed.

"Peaches, want a photo?" I asked. It seemed only right to commemorate his maiden voyage. He nodded, and Ariel pulled a Polaroid camera out of one of the dresser drawers and we took pictures of him, alone and with each of us. When he saw the first Polaroid his eyes got wide – for some reason he hadn't got-ten the whole picture of himself until he saw it in the photo, and he preened in front of the mirror every chance he got for the rest of the night.

"I knew the minute I saw you that you'd take to this," said Ariel, "but I'm going to curse myself forever for not doing your nails."

"Now what?" asked Peaches. It's a good thing there were sev-eral of us there – that boy really wanted an audience, and we were just barely enough.

"Well, we could go out," said Ariel, "and everyone could marvel at how gorgeous we all are, especially you. You could go turn a couple of tricks with me while these three go through the hors d'oeuvres I set out earlier. That would be fun. Or we could play the classic femme game."

"What's that?"

"Now that you're flawless, we all ravish you and try to fuck up your makeup."

"Did you use that porno star lipstick that doesn't rub off no matter how much head you give?" I asked.

"Of course I did."

"Really?" Peaches said innocently. "That kind of sounds like a challenge."

And just like that, Ariel's room went from Makeup and Wardrobe to the main set of a porno movie. Peaches dropped to his knees in front of Demetrius and went for his cock. He had obviously done Demetrius before – that or he deserved a special new position in Sir Sebastian's house. "Butler" didn't quite do justice to his special abilities.

And while his painted mouth slid skillfully up and down Demetrius' cock, his ass in that clingy skirt wiggled hypnotically. I couldn't tell whether he wiggled it on purpose or was throwing so much of himself into sucking cock that his whole body swayed, but the effect was the same either way – Peaches' ass, fuckable even at the most mundane of times, became irresistible.

Ariel saw the scene before it unfolded and swept the leftover lingerie off the bed. "I thought we might go through two or three changes of clothes," she said, "but I see now how unrealistic an idea that was."

"Is it okay that we're taking over your bedroom, Ariel?" I whispered. "We can go to mine if you want."

"Darlin,' it's not just okay, it is an honor."

Jack moved behind Peaches and, grasping his hips, gently pushed, making him and Demetrius move backwards towards the bed. When Demetrius's knees struck the mattress Jack said, "Lie back and let this flawless piece of ass work your cock, baby." To Peaches he said, "Up over the mattress, pretty boy."

Peaches didn't miss a stroke as Demetrius lay back, creeping up the side of the bed until he lay splayed over the edge. His skirt had worked itself up almost high enough to show us his cheeks. Jack ran his hands up the boy's thighs, lifting the skirt all the way up. He stroked Peaches' cheeks, parting them with his thumbs, and Peaches arched his back every time Jack spread him open.

Sweat ran in runnels down my body under the skin-tight latex. I found Ariel's condom stash and went for Jack's cock. It didn't need much stroking up once freed from his jeans. As soon as it got hard, I lubed it up for him. Ariel slipped in a deft hand to pull off Peaches' g-string. "This is why you put it on over your garters," she whispered to Peaches, but the time for fashion advice had clearly passed.

Jack sank his cock into Peaches in a long, slow, smooth thrust that make both of them moan out loud. Demetrius seemed to like the feel on his cock of the sound Peaches made – he thrust up, and before long they all kept the same rhythm, long slow strokes into Peaches's ass, long slow strokes down Demetrius' cock. For a minute Ariel and I just stood and admired the tableau.

Finally Ariel pulled off her panties and her shoes. "It's been a long time since I was in a bathhouse," she said, "but this reminds me of it." And she climbed up on the bed and knelt above Demetrius. Her offer was met with a long swipe of his tongue on her cock and balls, or big clit, or whatever she would have called it right at that moment, so she settled down on him so he could get it all in his mouth. I'd noticed before that Demetrius's mouth was, like the rest of him, big – but seeing it in action impressed me anew, because he could engulf all of Ariel's jewels at once, cock and balls and everything – they were just gone. Ariel didn't always get fully hard, though sometimes she did, but I figured that would just make her easier for Demetrius to suck. And seeing Ariel's equipment vanish that way, I ran for the Polaroid. I figured she'd want to see how she looked with her penis gone.

"What I love about small orgies," Ariel gasped, "is that they look like a perpetual motion machine devised to make Pee Wee Herman's toast or something. Pick a position and get on board,

Miranda."

It took me a few minutes to get situated, out of so much to choose from. I could reach everybody's tits; Jack's ass was available, and Ariel's; and I could get to Peaches' cock if I slid in sideways. But I knew the way Jack fucked. His strokes, slow now, would pick up in speed and force before long. "That's the other thing about small orgies," I muttered; "you can dislocate your jaw if you're not careful."

I didn't want Jack to shoot too soon, either, and if I played with his ass, he might. Ariel could go all night this way, though, so after I pulled on a latex glove and lubed up, I crept onto the one remaining corner of the bed and started working fingers into her, first one, then two and three. She shoved her ass back at me, partially pulling off Demetrius to do it. I responded by thrusting more firmly in, reassuring her that she didn't need to choose between her ass and her clit – she could have both at once.

From my perch at the head of the bed I could watch Jack plowing Peaches. He met each of Jack's thrusts with a back arch that incorporated a swivel of his hips, and when his hips went one way, his head went the other, so that now he went down and pulled off Demetrius in sort of a corkscrew motion. Jack grinned and rolled his eyes – this technique obviously had its effects. Meanwhile, Demetrius' hands roamed over Peaches, over Ariel, and discovered me. He tugged me closer in, and seconds later I felt his big fingers working their way into my cunt. He had just enough room for a slight, tantalizing thrust, but I didn't need much. I had the best view in the house, and besides, plugged into the perpetual motion machine, a little sensation went a long way. It *did* look like the baths, only a little heavy on the couture.

Ariel began coming first; with all the sensation from my hand and Demetrius' mouth, she soon started to buck and quake and yell. She could do that again and again, though, so I knew she wouldn't be ready to stop any time soon. Our orgasms weren't simultaneous, more like charges set to go off in a row. Peaches writhed and gasped, filled with cock. Jack slapped Peaches' ass, began the litany of dirty talk that almost always accompanied his come. "Pretty-ass fucking whore, boy-pussy, fucking little slut..." Hearing this turned up the volume for Peaches and pretty soon he had Demetrius shooting too. And once Demetrius began to go off, I swear the energy of his come zapped me through his hand, sending me into convulsive, intense thrusts as I rode his fingers. And that, naturally, got Ariel going once more.

It took us quite some time to disengage, even longer to remember to check Peaches' makeup to see if we'd managed to trash it. I finally made it to the kitchen for a jar of pineapple-mango juice to pass around. I brought it and the hummous tray back for a post-fuck picnic on Ariel's frayed old Persian rug. Peaches' makeup turned out to be a little the worse for wear, but Ariel did a much more watertight job than I ever did. She had all that professional stuff anyway. "I refuse to trick in anything else," she explained. "It has to be industrial-strength."

And sure enough, most of my makeup came right off later when they put me in the tub and pissed on me. Not that I cared. I was too busy jerking off, just like Jack told me to. Finally, under Miranda's girl-drag, my inner submissive was back. Or maybe it was just my inner pig. In any case, Ariel had been right about every fashion suggestion this evening. The latex hosed right off.

DRESS-UP, TAKE TWO

Ariel played me the phone message as soon as I got home. No "hello," no "goodbye," just Peaches' voice saying, "That was fun! Can we do it again?"

"I got the little tramp's phone number the other night," Ariel said. "Unless you're out with the boys tonight singing 'Don't Dream It, Be It,' we're gonna have Peaches over and sing 'Sweet Transvestite.'"

Since no public festival in Transsexual Transylvania could ever have matched my recent memory of the five of us on Ariel's bed, I said sure.

"I CAN'T BELIEVE that was the first time you'd ever done drag," Ariel said to Peaches. "Now that you're back in our clutches, you can do it as often as you want."

"I thought about it a lot," said Peaches, "but then I got my position over at Sir Sebastian's and there was just no place for it."

"Yes, it's like butch Disneyland over there, I expect," Ariel sighed. "It's a waste of good cheekbones, if you ask me. Now come on, let's head for the shower."

I think Ariel would have been a shower slut even without the need to do away with the stubble that had begun to mar Peaches' sleekness. She loved hot water, whether covering her up to the neck or pounding down like rain. Tonight she ran a little water into the tub, enough to get us wet and keep us warm. The razors hadn't been used up the other night, so after Peaches was slicked down with shaving cream, we went to work. It was far too much fun shaving Peaches to let him do it himself.

Ariel did his cock and balls, her careful hand efficiently swiping every tiny hair away. I finished his legs at the same time. When Ariel had selected a fresh razor and gone to work on his face, I filled my hands with a puff of slippery shaving cream and slid them between Peaches' thighs. This lather had nothing to do with shaving him closer – Ariel had done a perfect job. But my hands hungered for his hard, slick, naked cock, his hairless ass and silky balls. I slid over their curved surfaces, not even thinking yet about how it felt to him, just pleasing myself with the firm heft of his shaft, the malleable curves and tempting ass cheeks. "*Ohhhh*," he breathed, but until Ariel finished his face he couldn't move much. I tormented him with a slick hand job, watching him struggle to keep his hips from bucking.

"Bitch!" he said when Ariel let him go. But he didn't sound upset. It sounded more like an invitation to up the ante, so I got another handful of cream and stroked him faster. My other hand continued to explore, and when I found his hidden asshole, he spread his legs to let me at it. "Please, yeah, inside me!" he moaned, and so I slid in, his body hot and tight around my fingers.

"Thank god I got unscented cream," said Ariel, then took Peaches' chin in her hand again. "Sweetheart, does one come wear you out? I have big plans for you, and I don't want you falling asleep in the bathtub."

Peaches managed to assure Ariel that a come wouldn't slow him down. "Okay, Miranda, do him," she said, and that permission was all I needed. A couple of minutes later – during which Peaches managed to bend over and grasp the tub's edge so he could thrust and writhe but not fall, still leaving me full access to both his ass and his cock – he shot onto the white porcelain, decorated already with spatters of frothy lather.

Ariel turned the shower on and the boy rinsed off the foam. He looked sleek and somehow even more slender, and his cock – which had not yet completely lost its erection, and in fact didn't for the rest of the evening – seemed even bigger than it had before the shave.

"NOW WHAT?" asked Peaches, after his transformation at the hands of Ariel was once again complete. He swished his hips so the short, flippy skirt twirled and spun, no doubt caressing his cock as it moved.

"Well, this time we really should go out," said Ariel. "I can tell you really want a bigger audience, so we ought to go find you one. Then we can pick somebody up and play the femme game."

"The one with the lipstick?" Peaches had it down, looking eye-battingly innocent and truly devilish, all at the same time. This was a combination that would take him far.

FOR THE FIRST TIME in a long while Ariel and I headed back to the Black Rose, flanking Peaches on either side. I saw us turning heads as we walked down into the Tenderloin. Ariel and Peaches kept occupied with walking lessons – he'd done fine at home, but learning to go downhill in heels was, as Ariel said, "the graduate school of cross dressing." Ariel was determined to make Peaches graceful before we arrived.

Queens lip-synched on the Black Rose's tiny stage. A nearly full house had turned out to watch them, to wait for a turn to perform, or to trick. We found a small table by the wall, though, where the view was good. Peaches gazed at the performers, but Ariel and I looked around the crowded house for likely prospects.

"Nearly all the men come here for the queens," whispered Ariel. "Some of them want to play; some of them pay for it. You never know who's who, though most of the trannies here charge for their time. I see several men I've tricked with, but none I'd wish on beautiful Peaches."

"Peaches, do you see anybody?" I asked.

He looked around at the men who lined the long bar and dotted the audience. Some, especially the ones occupying tables, were already accompanied by queens. Others looked around, boldly or surreptitiously. "Everyone's on the make?"

"Baby, one way or another. Do you see Daddy?"

"As a matter of fact," said Peaches, holding a gaze over his shoulder, "I believe I do." My eyes followed his, and sure enough, there sat a well-dressed businessman, handsome, gray at the temples, and more self-assured than most of the men who surrounded him.

"He's perfect," said Ariel. "Looks like an out-of-towner, too. If you're lucky, he's in a hotel."

"If *we're* lucky," I said, "he likes voyeurs." But we'd know soon enough – seeing Peaches look at him, he'd risen and headed our way.

JOHN ONLY LIFTED an eyebrow when Peaches told him he wanted us to come along. He gave us the once-over, decided we weren't dangerous (which, as Ariel grumbled later, was a big assumption), downed the rest of his drink, and invited us back to a spacious room just a couple of blocks away.

Ariel and I hung back a few steps on the walk to the hotel. Peaches, as cool as could be, had laced his fingers through John's and leaned into him, murmuring – something seductive, no doubt. "John knows, doesn't he?" I whispered.

"Oh, he knows, all right. There's nothing on his mind right now besides Peaches' cock, except maybe that we've got cocks, too. This is a specialty thing, baby – guys don't find their way to the Rose who aren't hunting for it."

"Is he queer, Ariel?"

"Some flavor of queer, baby, but no one knows the first thing about these guys, except, in a way, us queens. No one pays any attention – not gay men, not their wives, not the sociologists. They want dick, but they don't want it on a man. They want a woman, but one whose cock they can suck. They're fetishists, they're bisexual – who knows? They know what they come out here looking for, even if nobody else does."

We drew some stares in the hotel lobby, but no one said a word to us. John carried himself with plenty of authority, and in fact, he seemed turned on by being seen with the three of us. By the time we were in the elevator his cock had risen to full erection. Peaches wasted no time, stroking it through John's trousers. I eyes it hungrily – it looked like one fine basket. I wondered if Peaches would share.

Ariel had something else in mind. She pulled Peaches' skirt up, revealing the newly-shaved cock and balls, heavy and pendulous, half-hard. It's a good thing John's room was on an upper floor and we were in a slow elevator, because he moaned and went to his knees, nuzzling Peaches' meat hard, swallowing it whole.

"See?" Ariel whispered, and my latex dress squeaked as I rubbed my clit.

I'VE ALWAYS LIKED WATCHING, but few scenes I'd ever been part of had the frantic heat of John's coupling with Peaches. Once we were in the room, Ariel locked the deadbolt and ordered John to strip. Expensive menswear went flying as he obeyed. Under it he had a truly gorgeous cock, straining hard, and a square, masculine body – real daddy material, all right. Peaches, quite fetched with him, seemed glad to let Ariel run the fuck. She ordered John to his hands and knees on the bed, then crouched in front of him, going eye to eye.

"I know what you want, John," she crooned. "This beautiful girl has a big hard cock for you, baby, and I know just where you want it." John whimpered. "Look at Peaches – you tell her what you want."

Peaches stood before John like a goddess. He flipped his skirt up and down, giving John peeps of his hard cock. It appeared and disappeared over and over. John didn't speak, though he didn't take his eyes off the place where Peaches' cock showed itself and vanished.

"John," said Peaches finally, "what did you bring me up here for? What do you want from me?"

John's moan was the only signal he might not feel as confident as he looked – at least, as he'd looked before Ariel got his pants off. But he finally managed, "Please...please – fuck me!"

"Your ass, baby?" Ariel prompted.

"My ass! Please, my asshole! Please – *fuck*!"

"Peaches?" said Ariel. "I've got a rubber right here." Peaches reached for it, but I hopped off the loveseat, where I'd been raptly watching, to put the condom on Peaches and then lube him up. I wanted that cock in my hands again – if anything, John's hunger for it made me want to touch it more than ever. When I let go, Peaches moved behind John, knelt, and nudged the man's asshole with his slippery cockhead. John immediately thrust back.

"Fuck his ass, baby!" said Ariel, and Peaches began working his hips in a mesmerizing rhythm, his cock sinking deep into John again and again. Every few thrusts, Peaches gave John a resounding slap on the ass.

I can get lost watching, and I could not tear my gaze away from this show. I felt each stroke of Peaches' hard meat as though he were fucking *my* ass. I imagined inhabiting John's big body, imagined ramming back to make each thrust deeper and harder. Peaches arched over John's body and filled the man's mouth with his fingers. John sucked, eyes closed, his loud moans communicating to me through my cunt. I filled my own mouth with my fingers, sucked, but never closed my eyes.

"Don't let him come!" Ariel's command broke my reverie, and Peaches pulled out a minute later when John was indeed getting close.

"On your back now, John."

He rolled over, panting, submissive. Ariel handed me

another condom.

"Do John's cock now, baby. We're going to watch Peaches get fucked." A sheen of sweat covered John, and his cock still strained tight against his muscular belly. As I handled him, it pulsed hotly. Peaches hovered over me, crouching so I could lube his asshole. I fingered its hot softness like I had earlier, got him open for the big meat he was about to take, then held John's cock upright so Peaches could poise his ass against the mushroom-shaped cockhead. John had the kind of cock that, once in, stayed, the head lodging behind the hole. Feeling Peaches' asshole against his dickhead, John humped up once, furiously, shoving in balls-deep. I had to pull my hand away fast, he went in so suddenly. But Peaches had no need for finesse. He let out a yell of pure fuck pleasure and began driving his hole down onto the thick cock as fast and hard as John could drive up into him.

I did not move away. I kept my face as close to them as I could. Peaches' ass stretched wide, and I could see the veins on John's cock straining as he pumped up and up into Peaches' hot ass, never slowing. I moved round them and caught John's nipples between my thumbs and forefingers, pulling them like reins. Still circling, I squeezed John's balls enough to make him cry out and hump even harder. I circled his cock as it withdrew from Peaches' hole, feeling its slick size, making sure the condom hadn't slipped. On every side I touched them, felt the fuck energy building, slid on John's sweat-sheened body, felt Peaches' muscles pump under his silky dress as he fucked onto John.

Ariel spoke again, still running it. "Randy, pull the dress off." I got up, managed to work the tight black knit over Peaches' head. "Take the bra off too." The boy's curved, solid chest emerged where the breast forms had been.

John's hands roamed over the newly-exposed flesh, the male pecs. He pinched the nipples, and Peaches reached for his. Pulling on each other's tits, riding like rodeo cowboys, both men yelled and growled as one come and then the other surged between them. Peaches' jism sprayed the other man's chest as John's last half-dozen humps up into Peaches filled the condom he wore. He bellowed, contorted, then went limp.

As Peaches relaxed onto John's chest, the bigger man's arms encircled him. I slunk my hand between them one more time, to pull John's softening cock free of Peaches' hole. While I was at it, I retrieved and tossed the condom.

THE FUCK DID JOHN IN.

Peaches dismounted, but John barely moved. We managed to drag the bedclothes halfway over him. Ariel sniffed. "That's an awfully inspiring degree of reliance on the kindness of strangers," she said. "Good thing he didn't pick up a working girl – he might lose his wallet. Baby, wash that come off your chest before you put my dress back on, okay?"

Peaches was only a little miffed that Daddy had turned into a pumpkin. He'd gotten what he came for, anyway. "I guess I'll just leave him a note," he said as John began to snore. "Call me next time you want a hot fuck, Daddy," he wrote on a card printed with his voicemail number. "Hmmmm, where can I leave it to be sure he'll find it? I know." He stuck the card to a pool of jizz, still viscous, on John's chest.

"He'll definitely find it in the morning," he said. Ariel beamed.

"I always wanted a little sister," she said, "and now I've got one!"

PLAY PARTY

Demetrius had big news next time I saw him and Jack. "Babies, that little spin we took the other night was just a dress rehearsal. Georgia Strong is coming through and Sir Sebastian is throwing a party in her honor – a mixed play party." We could hear the excitement in his voice. "Randy, you'll get to revisit the scene of the crime – as a woman! And you'll get to meet Georgia."

"Are you sure it'll be okay for me to go? What if Sir Sebastian's crowd figures out about last time? What if they give Jack a hard time?"

"Don't worry about that. St. James won't be there – he never plays in the same space with women, even Georgia. Any of the other guys who'd be freaked out – they won't be there either. And I'll handle Sir Sebastian if he makes a fuss – which he won't. Georgia's one of his dearest friends. For all I know, they're lovers, or used to be. He's hosted mixed parties before. It'll be okay."

"When is it?" Jack asked.

"In a couple of weeks. Gives us a little time to figure out what we want to do."

"Should I go femme or boy?"

"Femme, I think. But it better be a good outfit."

MAKE THAT A fabulous outfit. I enlisted Ariel's help, of course, and we reprised our favorite Opera Slut ensemble. It was a fitted leather dress, blood-red, with long sleeves, cut above the knee, but not too high. Not a conservative look, exactly – much too much red leather for that – but there was nothing especially fetishistic about its cut, and from the front it drew no more attention than any other really good-looking dress. The back was another story. It was completely open, from neckline to hem. It stayed on by means of a series of silver chains, spaced about three inches apart. In the center of each chain a tiny lock held the dress on. It had no other fasteners of any kind. My only lingerie, a matching red leather garter belt, also fastened with a lock and chain. I wore very tall red pumps, each with a two-inch platform and seven-inch heels. Black-seamed stockings, of course. At the opera I wore a sheer shawl with it, while Ariel sported a single key around her neck. At Georgia Strong's party I wouldn't need the shawl, and Jack would wear the key.

"You'd better have flawless makeup to go with this. You want to impress this Strong woman," said Ariel. "I've heard about her. She's supposed to be awesome. Remember what Sue said – you need more pussy in your life." I kicked her. "Besides, you know what happens at play parties. Everyone will try to fuck up your makeup. It has to be able to withstand anything."

"Maybe you could come along and bring your makeup kit," I said, only half-joking. "You can touch me up when I'm in the sling or after everybody gets done pissing on me."

"If you can get me an invitation and it's okay with the boys," Ariel said, "I'd love to come. I've been trying to figure out how to cross paths with Georgia Strong."

Since playing dress-up, Demetrius adored Ariel, and he thought the idea of my bringing her along to fix my makeup was a complete hoot. "Of course she can come," he said. "I was going to ask her anyway, as a matter of fact."

THE NIGHT OF THE PARTY Ariel locked me into my dress. "God knows who's gonna get you out of it," she said. She did my makeup so I barely recognized myself. She used her heavy-duty stuff – "Now just try to smear that off!" – and then she got dressed, in a deep-blue leather halter and miniskirt. Her four-inch pumps were nothing but a criss-crossing of tiny straps, and though I'd seen her in much higher heels, her legs went on for miles and miles anyway. When Demetrius and Jack rang and we went downstairs, they made us walk up and down the street a couple of times, showing off.

"That rear view is especially good," said Jack.

"Thank you, but may we get in the car now? I know it's amusing to walk us up and down like a couple of 'hos, but I *am* a 'ho and this is my night off."

Sir Sebastian had sent his car for us. As his driver headed across the Bay Bridge, Jack said, "Last time Randy came this way she was a blindfolded piece of pig-meat. Now we're all being treated like a bunch of dignitaries."

"Yes, a well-rounded life is the only life worth living," said Demetrius. "Sir Sebastian has very good brandy. Would anyone like a sip?" We all said yes and he poured cognac. "Waterford tumblers," he mused. "I'll bet Waterford pays the mortgage by selling tumblers to limo companies."

"Randy, how far apart can you spread your legs in that dress?" asked Jack. I showed him. "Hmm, that's not wide enough. Pull the dress up to your waist, please."

I obeyed. The three of them could now see my pussy, framed by the red leather garter belt.

"Much better. Now spread as wide as you can."

Again, I obeyed.

"It may take as long as a half an hour to get to Sir Sebastian's, depending on traffic," Demetrius said. "What are we going to do to keep entertained?"

"Masturbate for us, Miranda," said Jack. "Make it entertaining. Wait, hold out your hand." When I did as he instructed, Jack spit on my fingertips. "Rub my spit on your clit, cunt," said Jack. "Get it wet. Rub it good. Keep your legs spread so wide I can see right up your ass. I want you out of control. I want to see you put on a show."

"Want to know one of my professional secrets, baby?" said Ariel. "When somebody wants to see you get really lewd, that's a splendid excuse to pull out all the stops."

So I began to circle my clit, Jack's spit making my cunt shine in the low light of the car. Before long juice oozed from my crack, too, and I spread my lips and laved it everywhere. I scooted down to the edge of the seat, legs in the air, so they could see everything. When I had plenty of cunt-juice lubricating me I delved two left fingers into my pussy, then up my ass. I saved the right hand for my cunt, alternating sinking fingers in as deeply as I could and circling my clit, faster, then faster still.

"That's right, child. Fuck that ass for us. Let us watch you do it. Open it up for us so we can use it later," growled Demetrius. "We have some very big plans for you tonight, pretty girl."

"Maybe we should roll down the windows and let the truckers see in," said Jack. "Maybe we should pull off at the Army base and get your ass fucked by everybody we can line up."

He went on this way for a good ten minutes while I fucked myself into a frenzy, wanting more and more desperately for a big cock, or Ariel's hand, or something, to fuck me deeper and harder than I could fuck myself. When I began to whimper for it, Jack said, "No, slut, you just wait until we get you to the party, you'll get fucked real good then." The three of them continued to watch me and comment on my progress. Finally, as the driver slowed to exit the freeway, Jack reached in his jacket and brought out a bottle of lube and a fairly large buttplug.

"That's it, baby, you're almost ready. Now just slide this plug into your ass, that's it, up your butt. Lube it up good, baby, yes, my little slut can take it...slide it up, shove it, that's right, you can take it. We need your ass to be ready for anything, Randy, and when you put that plug up your asshole just remember, that's *my* cock sliding up your hole, that's *my* hole to use, be a good girl, shove it in..."

I could slide my ass down a fireplug when he talked to me like that. By the time we turned up Sir Sebastian's hilltop drive, the plug stretched my ass and sent jolts of feeling through me whenever the car hit a rut; but I had composed myself, to the degree possible. My skirt pulled down, my hands cleaned off, I sipped the rest of my cognac.

PEACHES MET US at the door. "Good evening, ladies, gentlemen." His eyes sparkled; the formality of his greeting veneered only thinly how glad he was to see us. Ariel didn't give a damn about formality, of course, so she kissed him on the lips. "Hi, baby," she said. "How's my pretty doll?" Peaches actually blushed at this, whispered, "Fine," took our coats and ushered us down the hall.

No more than twenty people had been invited to Mistress Strong's party. Besides Peaches and my companions I recognized only Sir Sebastian, who greeted us warmly.

Across the room stood a woman who could only be Georgia Strong. Dressed in a tuxedo with a swallowtail coat, she cut an even more imposing figure than I'd expected. She had all the presence Demetrius had described, plus a dignified beauty that gleamed forth from her masculine presentation like a jewel from a case. Her one concession to obvious femininity, her long and shining black hair, hung like a gleaming curtain down her back. It was streaked white at the temples. Her almond eyes glittered black, radiated intelligence, drew whomever she looked at into a spellbound respect.

I could see that Ariel was knocked out completely.

Peaches approached Georgia deferentially, careful not to disturb her conversation with a ravishing, Amazonian blonde.

When at length she turned to him, I saw that he had approached her to indicate our presence. She broke off her conversation at once and crossed towards us.

"Demetrius!"

That one word and he was in her arms. He held her tightly for a long time, wordless, and in the gesture were years of deep, complicated relationship underpinned by solid, simple love. I realized this tableau showed me Demetrius' soul, and that I already knew how deep and solid he could be: It permeated his relationship with Jack and, indeed, even with me. That Georgia Strong cherished him was equally obvious.

She had not met Jack, though she had clearly heard tales of him from Demetrius. She greeted him warmly.

"And this is Miranda, our boy" – Georgia's lips curled into an amused smile as Demetrius introduced me this way – "in whom I think you will take quite an interest, Georgia." Georgia reached for my hand and I inclined my head respectfully; when I raised it she met me with a grin, obviously willing to take Demetrius' word for it. "And our dear friend Ariel," he finished, but he didn't need to say anything more; Ariel was on her knees in front of Georgia, lips pressed to the back of her hand. She wasn't putting anything on, either – simply responding to the other woman's overwhelming presence.

"If there's anything you need tonight, Mistress..."

Georgia raised Ariel up. "Oh, I'll call you, my beauty," she said, "have no fear."

"This is just like Demetrius' story," I whispered to Jack.

"She's very used to it," he whispered back, as Demetrius, overhearing us, nodded. "She has this effect on a lot of people."

THE NEXT ARRIVAL, another of Georgia's old friends, took her away from us. "Go, play," she said. "We'll talk more later." I had a feeling I could expect exactly zero makeup assistance from Ariel, especially if Georgia really intended to call on her for anything. But that didn't matter. Getting your makeup trashed, while embarrassing, only means that the party's a success.

"Georgia's traveling with a master piercer," Demetrius said.

"Who? Star?" asked Jack. Even I'd heard of Star, through the grapevine. Star specialized in doing piercings under unusual circumstances.

"Yep. Who wants to get pierced?"

Jack and I looked at each other. We had talked about getting my nipples done. With twenty people in the room, we could cook up some very unusual circumstances indeed. "Randy...?"

I took a deep breath. "Sure, I'll do it."

"Jack, what about you?" asked Demetrius. "Want to do your cock?"

Jack looked thoughtful. Then he grinned. "If you can catch me standing still."

"Oh, I'll bet that can be arranged." Then he turned to me. "Randy, here's the deal. Jack and I want to have use of you tonight, and if you agree, Star will just decide which is the right time and do it. You won't see it coming." He chuckled. "The first nipple, anyway."

I nodded. The phrase "have use of you" got me wiggling on the buttplug.

"Okay, baby. Another wild ride." Jack gave me a squeeze, than caught Peaches' eye.

"Yes, sir?"

"Peaches, you know the enema set-up for guests, I assume?"

"Of course, sir."

"Take Miranda and get her ready, then, would you?" To me, but still audible to the boy, Jack said, "Honey, let Peaches do anything he wants to you, but be back within half an hour."

Peaches grinned and led me away. I was pretty sure that under his leather jockstrap his cock had begun to rise.

DOWN THE HALL we went, and into a vast marble bathroom.

Geez, Sir Sebastian seemed made of money. Peaches locked the door behind us and at first bustled about, very businesslike, getting my enema ready. The bathroom had a drawer full of individual chrome-plated nozzles for a silver bullet–style shower hose, and Peaches gloved up and screwed one on. "We have an autoclave in the utlity room," he explained. On the back of the toilet stood a pump bottle of lubricant.

"Peaches, I have a big plug in. I'm not sure I can get it out by myself."

Peaches grinned again. "Show me."

For as perfectly submissive as Peaches could be, the little devil could switch! This was good to know. I raised my dress, bent over the sink, and spread so Peaches could see the plug.

"Try to take it out."

I took hold of the plug's flange with both hands and pulled – awkwardly, because my hands were behind me and I had to pull backwards – and couldn't quite get the plug to dislodge. "I can't. Would you help me?"

"Sure." His grin burned my ass even though I had my back to him. He got the plug out with no trouble, though he took his time, fucking it in before he began to withdraw it. When it came out of my ass he dropped it calmly in the sink. I started to straighten up, but he put his hand on my asscheek and said, "Stay right there." I looked over my shoulder at him. "I like to look at your ass," he continued. "Do you know that I've never fucked a girl? I've wanted to, but I never have." As he talked he turned the water on and diverted it to the nozzle attachment, tested the water temperature, and lubed the nozzle itself. "And Jack said I could do anything to you, so I will. C'mere." He repositioned me in the shower, still bent over and legs spread, and slid the nozzle into my ass. It went in easily after the much bigger plug. Peaches carefully adjusted the water pressure, so I was being filled slowly.

"Tell me when you feel full." I did, and he turned the water off so I could dump the contents into the commode. "Now again." After two rinses I felt pretty clean, and told him so. "Once more," he instructed, "I want to make sure, and I want to try something Sir Sebastian did to me." This time when I told him I felt full, he turned the water off, said, "Stay there. Put your hands on the shower wall." A familiar foil-tearing sound alerted me when he put on a condom, and the next thing I felt was his hands on my hips, careful not to touch my rucked-up dress, and his cockhead at my cunt.

"Don't spill," he said, and rammed into me.

Demure Peaches was a thrashing, screaming fuck. Well, I screamed, anyway, from his hard thrusts and especially from the intense fullness of the water in my ass. He had me by the hips the entire time and moved me the way countless men had moved him, fucking his pretty and always-available butt.

He yelled his come while I fought to keep from coming, because if I came, I would spill. He pulled out and helped me to the toilet, where every last bit of fecal matter in me swooshed out, and as he cleaned up, still grinning, I said, "You owe me an orgasm, bitch!"

BACK AT THE PARTY, Jack and Demetrius smirked when we entered the room. "Better get back on duty, doll," said Demetrius, and Peaches quickly fell into service mode again, leaving my side with a quick "Just let me know when you want to collect."

Jack had staked out a low, sturdy table, one suitable for whipping, fucking, piercing, or just about anything that involved reclining. They led me there, and Jack held up the key that kept me locked into my dress. "Turn around, slut," he said. "You're overdressed." I did as he told me, and saw that while he unlocked me, Demetrius was also getting undressed. My clothes off, Jack removed his. In a room full of leather and fetishwear, we three stood out, naked except for their boots and my shoes, stockings, and the still-locked-on garter belt.

"Remember the cabinet where the clothes go?" Jack asked.

I nodded. "Take them, please."

When I came back, Jack sat straddling the table, stroking Demetrius's cock as the other man stood next to him. Desultory yet intensely, intimately erotic, they waiting for me yet stayed involved with each other. Somehow, a thought that would have hurt me only weeks ago – that they'd be fine even if I never came back – seemed almost reassuring now.

Seeing me, Jack lay back on the table. "Get my cock hard, baby." I knelt above him, took his cockhead in my mouth, sucking it almost immediately erect. He probably stayed soft by force of will just so he could tell me to make him hard. "Pussy wet enough for me?" he asked. "Get your cunt all the way down on my meat, then." I slid up his body til my pussy lips captured his cockhead, then shifted my weight and began sliding down. Inch by inch his big cock filled me. "Fuck me, girl," he said. "Do it, fuck me."

While I moved up and down, pinioned by his cock, Demetrius moved behind me. I felt the table shift when his weight settled on it, and feeling him there, leaned back into him. His big arms circled me. Centered on Jack's meat, held by Demetrius, I felt hot and loved. Feeling him begin to thrust against my back, I felt hotter still.

"Babygirl," murmured Demetrius, "I'm gonna go into your ass. Stay down on Jack's cock for a minute and don't move."

Demetrius' cock was huge. I had never had it in my ass. I didn't think I could. "Oh yes you can," hissed Jack, below me, supporting me so I could relax as the bigger man's cock slowly, slowly invaded. "I know what a pig you are. You could take my fist. Open up for him. You belong to us, you know. You wear our collar and you take our cocks and you'd drink our piss if we let you. Your ass is *not* closed to him. You'll fucking take his meat and you'll fucking love it!"

On my knees, in Jack's arms, legs spread so open I could not have stopped Demetrius had I wanted to, I drew a deep, shuddering breath and pushed back a little. It was barely a movement, but it did what Jack told me to do: acknowledge Demetrius's ownership of my ass. And from across the room, I felt the gaze of the woman who'd owned Demetrius. Without seeing her, I felt her approach.

"Little boy," she said to me, her voice cutting through my body's struggle to engulf the big cock. "Look at me."

I managed to meet her eyes, though I had to twist my neck to do it.

"I was Demetrius' master once. When I bent him over any surface, he knew he had to open to me. When he didn't think he could, I told him he must. And I can see that you are quite as devoted to these men as he has been devoted to me. Breathe. Take him."

So I breathed. With every exhale, Demetrius pushed in further. He never relented, nor did he shove or hurt me. I lost track of time, of myself, of everything except my body being filled with ownership, and with love.

He was in. But he wasn't finished. Slowly, slowly he began to move, and as he did, Jack, who had been still the whole time I struggled to take Demetrius, moved with him.

Impaled like this, Demetrius pulled me up so that my body arched back, curving up over Jack like the figurehead of a ship. "Pretty," he breathed, "very pretty. Fuck our girl, baby." And Demetrius fucked. He didn't stop until he saw Star approaching.

Star came gloved and ready. He smiled, swabbed my nipples with antiseptic, said, "Stay still," and with a practiced eye caught my left nipple in clamping hemostats. Any other time this would have hurt me, but not with Demetrius ballsdeep in my ass. The needle tugged, the ring burned, and as if from a great distance I heard Jack say "Yesss."

Star repeated the process on the right side. A trickle of blood adorned one breast.

"Beautiful, Star," came Georgia's voice. "Good boy, Randy. Jack, Demetrius, she's yours."

Cocks moving simultaneously said "We know," as eloquently as if they'd spoken the words. Their cocks alone chained me to the earth.

PEACHES HAD MOVED CLOSER when first Jack, then Demetrius, came. I felt like the whole scene, once both cocks were in me, had been one long orgasm. Peaches accompanied us back to the big bathroom, drew us a bath, and left us there. A few minutes later he returned with a carafe of ice water and a tray of hors d'oeuvres.

"Peaches doesn't miss a trick," I said fuzzily.

"I'll trick with you any time," he said, and disappeared.

Unbelievably, the bath and the food replenished me. We returned to a party in full swing – literally; at midnight the "Hallelujah Chorus" started, and the beat infused every scene. Spankings, whippings, floggings, even fucks shared the beat of the music, cries melded with the recording, orgasms happened in time to Mendelssohn. I wondered if anyone before me had thought to sing "For Georgia Strong, omnipotent, reigneth."

Her Omnipotence reigned over Ariel this evening. Ariel, lashed to the St. Andrews cross, arched up to meet whipstrokes. Interspersed with strokes from Georgia's hands, they sang down in a torrent of "Hallelujah! Hallelujah!" And I could see that Ariel rejoiced, all the way across the room.

"THE SLING IS EMPTY," said Jack.

"Amazing. Get it."

Jack hoisted himself into the fine leather sling, letting his ankles rest in the loops that were hung at just the correct height. He looked around for Peaches, who appeared at the right moment with gloves and Crisco. "Peaches, you're unbelievable."

"Thank you, sir." Now that he had fucked all of us, Peaches's formal demeanor covered a rather charming smirk. I guessed that he did it on purpose, angling for a beating from Jack or Demetrius or both.

I gloved up and began working my hand into Jack's ass.

With the Crisco it was easy – besides, fucking Demetrius regularly was almost like getting fisted by me. I started with three fingers and worked quickly up to four. When I began to push in with all five, fingers bunched together in a point to make entry easier, Jack began to moan and rock the sling, thrusting his ass against me.

"He's a butt slut, that boy," said Demetrius. "No doubt about it." And indeed, I'd only been at it for a few minutes and Jack had just about swallowed my hand. A couple of minutes later, my hand went in.

"He's a little difficult to impress, actually," said Demetrius. "Tell you what, Randy, let's work him over together." He double-condomed his dick, using the largest rubbers on the tray Peaches had left – they still didn't cover the entire shaft – and slid his cock into Jack's ass – with my hand already inside! "Open your hand as much as you're able, Randy," he said, "so I can fuck your hand inside his ass."

This got Jack's attention.

"Baby, Randy's jerking me off, up your ass," said Demetrius. This was not really accurate – in fact, he fucked my hand, which couldn't move enough to jerk him off. But whatever you called the movement, it made Jack soar. He moaned, shoved his fully-opened hole against us to get us a tiny bit deeper, growled and drooled.

"This is where we used to bring out the poppers," Demetrius whispered. "You think he's a pig *now*."

Orgasms rolled through Jack, convulsive waves we felt from the inside. His heart beat hard; my wrist ran along one of his arteries, which throbbed with each rush of blood. I felt my own heart keeping time.

Star appeared. Peaches, at his side, held a tray with his piercing gear.

Star swabbed Jack's soft cock just as he had done my nipples. Holding it in his hand like a small sleeping animal, he selected a curved needle from the tray and marked the place the needle would emerge for a Prince Albert. I remembered Jack telling me how hot a piercing he thought the PA was. Another orgasm rippled though him at the handling of his cock.

"Be very still now, Jack," said Star. Demetrius and I stayed totally still. Peaches, with his free hand, held Jack's hip. Demetrius stabilized the other.

Star gently threaded the needle partway down Jack's urethra. Again he gauged the spot the piercing would emerge. Then, with a flick of the wrist, it was done.

Jack growled and writhed, the sensation of the piercing mingling with an orgasm. The sling shook.

When he fell still again Star threaded the ring, a solid twelve gauge, through the piercing, tightened the bead closure, and was done. "Keep it clean," he said. "Careful when you come out of his ass."

Which we had to do soon, because of the way Crisco eats gloves.

LATER, ALL OF US – except Ariel – were back in our clothes, piercings bandaged. Peaches served us tea in Georgia Strong's guest room. I lay back in Jack's arms dreamily – careful not to press up against his dick – and Ariel curled up at Georgia's feet. Georgia and Demetrius talked.

"It's so good to have you back here," he said. "Will you stay?"

"I think for a bit," Georgia said, glancing down at Ariel. "It's possible that I'll open an office here again. There seem to be women in town with some potential for maintaining it for me while I'm away."

"The Hong Kong office?"

"I may move it to Singapore. I'm weighing my options."

The business talk made me sleepy. I sighed deeply in Jack's arms. But Demetrius' next question woke me up.

"So what do you think of my friends?"

Georgia smiled. "I think you have family here, not just

friends."

"True."

"I was momentarily surprised to see you with a woman."

"Things are always more complicated than they seem at first glance. Also simpler. You taught me that."

"I did."

"And you taught me that there are layers of truth, and of experience. That I could live in my body and my desire exactly the way it is. That if I'm willing, I can have what I want. She has that too, Georgia."

"Demetrius, everyone you ever choose will have that."

THE LETTER

Not long after the party, as Demetrius packed his bags for a short trip to New York to see his son, he called me over to his place. Jack lounged on Demetrius' bed, still careful how he arranged his body because of the piercing. "Hey, doll," he said when I entered.

"Hey, Jack. Hi, Demetrius. What's up?"

"I've thought of an entirely new adventure to keep you occupied while I'm out of town and Jack's dick is in a splint, that's what's up," said Demetrius. "Now that we've taken this much responsibility for your social calendar, we can't just be leaving you idle for days at a time. Lord knows what you'd go dragging home."

"I'll be good!" I said. "You don't have to keep me occupied, either, unless you want to."

"Oh, darlin,' this is a *big* 'want to.' Here." Demetrius held out an envelope.

"Demetrius, this is addressed to Georgia Strong!"

"Yes, and that's *Mistress* Georgia strong to you, upstart, unless she tells you to call her something different."

"Yeah, like 'Mommy,'" said Jack. "Or 'Sir.'"

Obviously the guys had decided to send me on a joyride, and they couldn't have picked a hotter, scarier, or more alluring one.

"So, dear, tomorrow at noon you're going to show up at the address on this envelope. Wear very upscale girl drag, please, and give Georgia the letter. She'll let you know what you are to do next."

I managed a nod, though my mind and cunt both burned, and tucked the letter safely into my jacket.

"Don't wear that ratty fucking thing," said Jack.

"Of course not," I said.

"Oh, and Randy? Remember every last teeny tiny detail. Jack and I will be looking forward to hearing all about it after you come crawling home."

"I'd go with you just to watch," said Jack, "but I have a feeling you should go alone. So it can just be – what do you call it? – 'women's space.'"

NOON THE NEXT DAY found me in the luxurious marble lobby of a downtown hotel. When I asked for Georgia Strong at the front desk they phoned up to make sure I could be admitted, then sent me to the penthouse. Hands shaking even though I tried to control them, I rang the bell.

Ariel answered. This did not surprise me, for I had seen neither hide nor hair of her at home since the party, and I'd already figured she'd run away from home to join Georgia. Given her long and checkered career, where else could she run to? The night streets of the Tenderloin were twice as exciting as the circus, and the costumes were almost as good. It would take something even more exciting than that to get Ariel's attention, and Georgia was obviously it.

Georgia had her elegantly tricked out in one of those very feminine lady-CEO power suits. Expensive pumps I'd never seen her wear caressed her feet with supple Italian leather. So they'd gone shopping already. Perhaps this was going to be serious.

"Hi, baby," she whispered. "So you found your way over."

"Yeah, the generals posted me here. How does this work? Do I give you the letter to deliver, or what?"

"Actually, I think you should present it to her yourself." Oh, right. With a thrill I remembered Demetrius' story about being sent with a letter to Sir Sebastian. My plum-colored silk suit rustled in the silence, and I fought hard to control my trembling as Ariel gestured me in.

Georgia sat at a simple table near a window. She had a deluxe executive day-minder in front of her, and a phone. At my approach she rose. "Dear Miranda, hello."

"Good afternoon, Mistress Strong," I managed, heart fluttering. "Demetrius sent me to deliver this, with his regards."

"Thank you." She took the clean cream-colored envelope, which I'd been very careful not to soil or wrinkle, and opened it. While she read it I glanced around the gorgeous Japanese-styled room, which gleamed with polished teak and rosewood. Stylized ikebana arrangements sported one flower each, and part of the room was screened from view by a series of rice-paper panes. Suddenly I felt far from San Francisco – even, in spite of Ariel's presence, far from my old life.

Georgia smiled as she put down the letter. "Miranda, do you know what this says?"

"No, Mistress Strong."

"Demetrius and Jack have been so kind as to give you to me for a negotiable period of time. Tell me, when do you next have responsibilities? A job to report to, for instance?"

"Monday morning, Mistress Strong." It was Saturday now. "And if I needed to, I could perhaps call in...I have leave accrued..."

"The old, 'Boss, I'm all tied up at the moment' routine? We don't operate that way around here. But thank you for your flexibility."

In fact I had quite a bit of leave accrued. I wondered if I should just call in now and say I'd be in a bit late...say, two weeks late. But that's just my inner pig talking, I reminded myself. Did I really want to lock myself up for two weeks with Georgia Strong?

Seating herself again, Georgia had to sweep her long gleaming hair back to keep from sitting on it. She evoked such feelings of loyalty, almost reverence – at least, from the people in my tribe. Today, for me, her gender seemed a null, a promise, a projection screen; neither masculine nor feminine, or perhaps both at once – but no less erotically powerful or compelling for the confusion I felt when I looked at her. Yes, locking myself up with her seemed like the best idea ever. This must be how Ariel had felt when Georgia took a shine to her: it felt like having a new lease on life. Not that I need one, given how busy Jack and Demetrius had been keeping me, but the plain fact remained: Somebody like Georgia Strong walked through your life only once.

"MIRANDA," SHE SAID. "Clothes off, please. You can hand them to Ariel."

I stripped. Ariel appeared at my side to take the silk suit. Being without clothes felt natural to me, but next to Ariel in her CEO drag and Georgia, who also wore power clothes, I felt very naked indeed. With every stitch draped over Ariel's outstretched arm, I suddenly remembered my posture and stood up as straight as I could. Muscles tight, shoulders back, my breasts stood out. A crazy thought followed: My nipples were a few inches closer to Georgia than the rest of me.

"Thank you. Miranda. Now, if you'll excuse me for a bit, I have some work to finish up before I can give you my full attention; please get on that window seat to my right, so I can look at you. Stand, please. Legs spread. You needn't hold yourself rigidly – stay relaxed and you'll be able to stand longer. If I have you for only forty-five hours, I certainly will require your endurance."

I obeyed, climbing into the recessed window. It had enough room for me to stand with my legs spread, as she had instructed, and, just like in Demetrius' story, San Francisco could look up my ass. Perched many stories in the air, I felt myself get wetter and wetter, glad that it was daylight and anyone who cared to look up would have something to see.

Georgia made a few calls and took some notes. She seemed to be moving fast on the San Francisco office, and more than once she conferred with Ariel. After nearly an hour she looked up at me – my platform put me a little above her, like a sculpture on a pedestal, the better to be examined when Georgia desired – and told me to turn around. Now, with my back to her, I could see out, see tiny cars driving and tiny people scurrying below, could imagine I saw one or two stop and stare up for moments at a time.

"You do seem to take to this," she said at last. "That tells me a good deal about you, Miranda. Step down now, please." When I obeyed, she said, "Now kneel on the seat cushion, facing the window. Legs spread as wide as you can get them. Good."

I could not see her and did not dare look behind me, but I heard fabric rustle as she removed some article of clothing. Seconds later I felt her hands on me, taking hold of my ass cheeks, spreading them, and then a cold, wet dribble of lube. I braced as well as I could on the padded ledge. No sooner had I clutched the edges of the cushion than I felt the tip of her dildo at the mouth of my hole. Its push in, steady and inexorable, felt like heaven – or just a little bigger. Her hands on my hips pulled me back even as she thrust in.

Georgia's cock soon eclipsed any other reality, She used it to make people hers, I dimly realized, to prove her possession and sustain it. She used it to please herself, too, for her thrusts were so hard and fast that they had to be turning her on, maybe bringing her up to orgasm. Unlike the men I had been fucking, she stayed virtually silent, all still fury and control. Soon she had me pressed up all the way against the window, tits against the cold glass (which felt wonderful on my still-tender piercings), hands clawing it uselessly for a hold. She caught hold of my shoulders and used the leverage to fuck me down hard, harder and faster, onto her cock. I screamed, swore, begged, prayed – not for mercy, but for her to drive me all the way out of my mind this way, for her to drive herself as deep into me as she could get. In her possession of my ass with the cool devil-prick dildo I was the one who'd lose control, not Georgia.

Georgia was tall, easily six one. She had more strength than any woman I'd ever known. She picked me up from the ledge, impaled on her cock, one arm around my waist and one around my shoulders, lifting me away from the window. She turned, holding me this way, and sat on the ledge where I'd just knelt, me on her lap now, her cock still buried deep in my guts, keeping me pinned against her. My feet could just reach the floor. Ariel sat in the chair she had vacated, watching, a new Ariel I didn't quite know. Her eyes on me made me feel very, very exposed.

"Fuck this cock with your ass. Fuck it as hard as it just fucked you," Georgia ordered. I had to struggle to keep my balance. I fucked until my thighs were aching and sweat streamed into my eyes. My clit felt huge, untouched this whole time. Her cool orders isolated me, an effect that was just the opposite of what I felt when Jack devoured me with his dominance, and I fucked more and more wildly to try to reach her.

"Ariel," said Georgia, "come over here. I want you to spit on your hand and work this girl's clit until she can't stay on her feet any more."

Ariel did exactly as she was told. She had worked my clit a thousand times, but this time it felt different from any other time we'd ever made love. Maybe because this time we weren't making love: we were making something for Georgia.

I LAY IN A SWEATY, fucked–out heap on the floor. Georgia looked down, not quite disapprovingly. "Miranda, you'll have to be able to take much more than that. You're a little bit spoiled, I fear. *Two* daddies." I looked up at her fuzzily, knowing I'd have to pull myself together if I didn't want to get thrown looking like this into the Nikko elevator, emerging in the marble lobby like something the cat dragged in. Besides, I couldn't bear the idea that I might displease her, that she might turn her back on me.

I managed to get to my knees. I'd been fucking with the big boys lately, but she was a tornado. "What can I do to please you, Mistress Strong?" I finally whispered.

"Hmmm, draw us all a bath, I think." She indicated a shoji-screen. Behind it I found a room-sized Japanese bath. I fumbled in its low light for a minute, figuring out where the taps were; I even found a screened cabinet full of towels, and I laid out three. She *had* said, "Draw us *all* a bath."

Out in the main room Ariel had removed her fancy CEO dress and busied herself helping Georgia disrobe. What Demetrius had never seen emerged before me: Georgia Strong, all six feet plus of her, slender but every bit of her muscled. The muscles ran and rippled under her skin like a wild cat's, elegant and powerful. Her small breasts hugged her chest, their softer planes not detracting from the effect of strength. While Ariel hung up her suit, Georgia knotted her long hair onto her head and secured it with a pair of ebony chopsticks.

The hot water of the bath relaxed me, started to clear my head, and again I tried to imagine what Georgia might want me to do. She allowed me to sponge her and Ariel, laving their bodies, which left me hungry to put my hands on her – but that seemed impertinent.

"Ariel, sweet beauty, how would you like to arrange for a meal?" Georgia said at last. "Call it up from downstairs, if you like. I don't expect we'll want to go out any time soon." Ariel left the bath; I could hear her as she called room service. Georgia turned to me. "That really left me feeling very unfinished. Miranda, come take care of that, please."

I couldn't quite believe what I thought she meant. Georgia sat on the edge of the tub, fine long legs spread. "Right here,

Miranda," she said. "You understood me the first time." And she gestured to her sex, her mound trimmed short, her clit protruding a little, the vulva lips a dusky plum, almost the color of my silk suit and looking just that silky. Kneeling to her, I moved my mouth toward her; when I got close she took me by the cheeks and put me exactly where she wanted.

I've sure I've made it plain that I love sucking cock, but nothing could ever compare to the feeling of her pussy filling my mouth succulently, her clit connecting electrically with my upper lip, her cunt ripe and juicy for my tongue to lap, soft where my teeth gently came together, asshole just below it all, and wouldn't you know my tongue found that too, wanting to give her everything just as she had taken everything from me – and wanting too to make a connection with her she couldn't deny, couldn't stay aloof from. She kept her hands on my face, guided me as I licked and sucked, burrowed and nibbled, slicked my face with her salty arousal. Her comes were quiet but obvious, all tight muscles and spasming release. I went at her until she stopped me, wanting to give her as much pleasure as she would take. I did not touch myself, though I suppose I might have, and I did not try to enter her with my fingers – if she had wanted that from me I knew she would tell me to do it. The greatest liberty I took, putting my tongue in her ass, filled my cunt with peppery heat, as I worked my way into her tightness as deeply as I could. By the time she lifted my face away, having had enough, more was slick than just my cheeks. I had to wash again, though I had been in the water all along.

Ariel had set out enough sashimi and rolled sushi to feed an army, but I hadn't counted on my own hunger after that workout. We all feasted. Georgia fed both of us from her own plate, dipping the pink fish into wasabi and burning us with it. This did exactly nothing to ease my cunt's burning.

EVENING FELL, darkening the windows, spangling with city lights our view from the high penthouse. Georgia instructed

Ariel to roll a futon into a bolster shape. She ordered me to lie over it. She bound my hands and fastened my ankles to a spreader bar, one of the most lewd of S/M devices. This position both exposed and immobilized me, and I did not know whether to expect blows, the softness of a tongue, a hand in my ass, or another of Georgia's furious sodomizings. I did not dare to try to peek behind me to see what might be coming, and she left me there for what seemed like a very long time, waiting, feeling her and Ariel's eyes on my spread-open holes.

There followed the whipping of my life, which I got for no reason except that Georgia wanted to do it. She started with her hands, spanking my ass hot and pink. It made me desperate for her hands or mouth on my clit, but she did not care, of course, what I was desperate for. After twenty minutes, she put a butt plug into my ass, which made the spanks' sting transmute into pure sexual sensation. She left the plug in, moving next to a paddle which thudded against me like a new way to get fucked. I knew the rain of blows had begun to mark me. I felt red welts raise, and I lost track of the border between pain and pleasure.

"Ariel, fuck her for me," Georgia said after one particularly heavy thwack had made my asshole tighten down hard and my back arch. So Georgia took a rest from hitting me while Ariel's clever, familiar hands moved in, one wiggling the plug enough to send waves of sensation through me, the other burrowing into my cunt, first two fingers, then three. She brought me to the edge of a big come, but stopped immediately when Georgia said, "That's enough." My old lover had become something for Georgia to torment me with, and I wondered in a rush of panic and pain whether she did not want to touch me herself.

More blows from the paddle. Each strike sent red waves of deeply erotic pain through me. Just as I verged on losing it to the intensity of the blows, they stopped. Next, Georgia pulled the butt plug out and used my ass again, even more ferociously now that I was spread out and shackled to the spreader bar, ass in the air, nowhere to go, nothing to do but take it. She had not given me a safe word, either. After every few deep, pounding strokes of her cock – she was still slamming into me without making a sound herself, though by now I sobbed and screamed – she slapped my ass hard, then grabbed the reddened, sensitized flesh of my ass-cheeks to spread me farther for her, I think just so she could more easily see the pornographic vision of my asshole spread so wide and filled so full of her. Georgia, I dimly realized, got a kind of intellectual pleasure out of this that equalled or even exceeded her pleasure in the body. She did it and watched it simultaneously. And I found there was a parallel pleasure for me, knowing that I was the one she chose to use. I began to hope I would not come, so that I could stay suspended on the intimate tight wire of need she had forced me out upon.

After sodomizing me she repositioned the butt plug and hit my ass again, with several repeated blows that fell on both cheeks simultaneously. Then she told Ariel to resume fucking my cunt. More fingers this time, and I felt her stretch me wide and wider as Georgia oversaw. I silently begged her to keep her eyes on my cunt, keep watching how much I wanted what she let me receive, how much I would take for her pleasure.

Ariel added more lube and worked her hand in deeper. The whole hand – of course she would go for the whole hand. She stretched my cunt unbearably wide; her hand was big, as big as Jack's. I tried to fight my own panic with deep, slow breaths. I wanted to show Georgia and Ariel that I could take it. "Don't let off, Ariel, keep pushing," Georgia commanded, and I begged them please, please to take me, to use me, to make me, make me take it, make me fucking take more, *more.*

At the widest point of Ariel's big hand, when I thought I would scream aloud with the intensity, Georgia started working my ass with the paddle again, with hard rhythmic blows that promised not to stop until my cunt was satisfactorily full. My yells sounded oddly quiet in the big room, and Ariel's hand took an eternity to slip inside, but they had made me take it. When her fist finally filled my cunt, I floated high above myself.

Now Georgia dealt me blows while in front of me, her cunt in my face, my mouth sucking her like a kitten sticks to its mother, her spanks still raining upon me from the opposite direction so she wouldn't interfere with Ariel's entry. And Ariel worked her fist inside me, every subtle motion feeling huge, every cell of me bound and spread and used according to Georgia Strong's wishes. Even through crying, screaming climaxes I felt peaceful, cared for – for they had given me what I begged for, had made me take what I could not – and I felt so very sexy. If a creature like Georgia wanted to watch her cock pound my asshole, watch lube froth up around the tender rim from the force of her fuck, then every bit of me must be beautiful, desirable. I could not have been happier – unless she had turned around and let my tongue go for her ass.

I SLEPT ON THE SAME FUTON she had stretched me over to beat me, my dreams half-remembered and wild. At least once I woke up coming.

The next day I watched Georgia make love to Ariel, for that is what it was, even when it seemed harsh or painful. Ariel teetered between being submissive (and goofy) as a new puppy and being raised even higher in dignity and self-possession. Georgia was clearly very good for her.

And Georgia talked to me, helped me understand who I was to Jack and Demetrius, who they were to me. I saw why she, really so deeply womanly, did not project gender with me – even with her cunt in my mouth. For me, gender was really not the important thing. For Demetrius, on the other hand, at the moment in his life when he had found her, it had been everything.

In the evening they took me to the hotel bar, without panties on, of course, and with my ass filled by the butt plug. I drank champagne and flirted with the traveling businessmen who had come down for a nightcap. When I had someone's full attention, Georgia motioned him to follow us to a well-lit alcove off the bar. There she ordered me each time to raise my dress and bend over, showing him my naked sex, the plug stuffing my ass, the welts and stripes from the beating. Georgia said that if any of them displayed a useful mixture of deference and hunger, she would bring him up to our room to use me.

But none of them did. A whole roomful of men failed to earn the right to me, though I was ready to be taken by any one of the lonely strangers who sat surreptitiously watching us. One by one Georgia picked them out, displayed me, offered me. One by one, timid or arrogant, they failed.

In the end she used me herself, of course, sitting once more on the window seat, her cock deep in my cunt as I sat on her lap facing her. Wrapped in her arms, lights twinkling over her shoulder, Ariel at our feet working fingers up my ass, I felt as happy as I'd ever been, though I cried and cried. My face buried in her neck, her veil of black hair silken under my lips, I came again and again, and she did not tell me to stop.

When she fucked Ariel she bent her over the writing desk and allowed me to burrow between her legs again, tongue pulsing with hunger for her cunt, working again as deeply as I could get up her hot ass, and this time I worked my clit desperately, furiously.

WORK WAS SLOW ON MONDAY, thank god, and I scrambled to try to write down what had happened to me at Georgia's. I feared I would lose the memories of it if I didn't. But I found that I couldn't find the right words to describe it: what it had meant to me.

Maybe when I told it to Jack and Demetrius the words would come.

MY FIRST RIDE

I felt restless, but Jack's dick was still broken. The PA looked so hot, it frustrated me not to be able to touch it.

I had been hanging out at Jack's, but he felt like reading in bed. Demetrius had left town for a few days. I prowled around his apartment trying to stay out of his way. I knew I should just go home, but I didn't feel like it.

"Randy!" At Jack's call I scurried to his room. "You can handle a bike, right?"

I could, but I couldn't quite believe my ears. "The Harley?"

"Yeah. Get your helmet. Then come back here."

In the hall, where the helmets were, stood a package with my name on it. I brought it back along with the helmet. "Jack..."

"Sure, open it."

Inside I found a box with a leather jacket in it – not a ratty one, like mine, but smooth new leather.

Jack didn't look up from his book. "Leave that fucking skanky-ass old jacket of yours at home from now on, okay?"

"Um, sure, Jack."

"Go put your leathers on and get back here." I did what he

said, reappearing in my chaps, vest, and the new jacket. "Good. Now catch."

He threw me the keys to the Harley. I caught them in midair, still not entirely getting it.

"My dick doesn't work," he said. "I'm bored. You're bored. Why don't you go see if you can find us a snack?"

"You mean...?"

"You know what I mean. A trick. A bounce. Bring him back and let's see what kind of mischief we can get into. Put on a show for me, or something."

"Why not just call Peaches?"

"Nah. I figured it's about time for you to learn to play a new game. Bring Daddy A Snack. Take the bike. You won't believe how boys flock to that bike."

CAREFULLY I POISED MYSELF, balancing on the handlebars, ready to bring my weight down on the starter. The rich, unmistakable Harley growl told me I had gotten it right the first time. Good, because Jack could hear me from his room right over the street.

I gunned it and pulled out of the alley. I circled around the few blocks that put me onto Folsom. How many leathermen – and not a few women – had sailed around that corner on how large a fleet of chromed, gleaming bikes, hunting for something?

The baths were gone. Most of the bars were gone. But men still filled the streets some nights, and even on slow nights one or two ghosted out of alleys. We were still here.

Across the street from Blow Buddies I parked and watched the comings and goings. It was so close to Jack's I could have walked over here. But the bike got attention – I saw men looking.

One looked again and again. He didn't go right into the club. He saw me, plus he seemed hesitant to enter alone. If it wasn't for the fucking dick check, I could lock up the bike and go in with him.

He went in at last, but he didn't stay in long. He hurried out, in fact, looking back over his shoulder. He saw me looking and straightened up, seemed to debate crossing the street and walking my way.

A small guy. Neat, very nice leathers. Probably new. Couldn't see his face too well from where I perched in the shadows. I sat there studying his walk.

Hmmm. I wonder.

As he stepped off the curb, I started the bike.

AFTERWORD

Grateful thanks to the 'zine and anthology editors who hosted early versions of the chapters that make up *The Leather Daddy and the Femme*.

John Karr, sex club doorman extraordinaire (and porn reviewer emeritus) fielded my call as to whether Blow Buddies ever implemented dick checks; okay, so I made that part up. Karr found the idea pretty amusing. Absolutely no disrespect meant to the West Coast's finest blowjob emporium – and I don't mean Collingwood Park.

Thanks are due to the many people who inspired me to spin the fantasies in this tale: San Francisco's beautiful tranny whores; all the hot butch girls who (at least sometimes) will be boys; the redhead who loaned her hair to Bella (and for whose tresses my hands still ache); these last two generations of queer men, out in the bathhouse and out in the streets, and the women unladylike enough to draw erotic inspiration from them; and of course the leather daddies, too many to count at the Folsom Street Fair.

The message I take away from the strong reader response to

these stories is that a lot of us want more of what Randy and her friends have. To the readers who urged me to keep telling the tale after "After the Light Changed" – you, too, are part of this tribe.

If only Cynthia Slater and David Lourea had lived to read this, to know that the torch has been passed. I write – and fuck – in their memory.

– CQ

ABOUT CAROL QUEEN

Carol Queen is a widely published author of erotic fiction, personal essays, and information about sexual enhancement. She is the author of *Exhibitionism for the Shy* (Down There Press) and *Real Live Nude Girl: Chronicles of Sex-Positive Culture* (Cleis). The original edition of *The Leather Daddy and the Femme*, published in 1998, won a Firecracker Alternative Book Award. Queen is co-editor of *PoMoSexuals: Challenging Assumptions About Gender and Sexuality* (which won a Lambda Literary Award) and *Switch Hitters: Lesbians Write Gay Male Erotica and Gay Men Write Lesbian Erotica* (both with Lawrence Schimel). She edited *Sex Spoken Here* (Down There Press) with Jack Davis and two volumes of *Best Bisexual Erotica* (Circlet/Black Books) with Bill Brent. Her educational videos *Carol Queen's Great Vibrations: An Explicit Consumer Tour of Vibrators*, *Bend Over Boyfriend: A Couple's Guide to Male Anal Pleasure*, and *G Marks the Spot: The Good Vibrations Video Guide to the G-Spot* are available from Good Vibrations, where she works as Staff Sexologist. Queen has a Ph.D. from the Institute for Advanced Study of Human Sexuality.

She and her partner Robert Morgan Lawrence are currently developing The Center for Sex & Culture, a non-profit sex education organization. She and Robert live in San Francisco with Teacup and Bracelt, the cats who own them.

More information about Carol Queen, including upcoming appearances, a full bibliography, and some of her work, is on the web at www.carolqueen.com.

OTHER BOOKS FROM DOWN THERE PRESS

Photo Sex: Fine Art Sexual Photography Comes of Age
    ed. David Steinberg $35.00

Anal Pleasure and Health, 4th Edition
    Jack Morin $17.95

The Good Vibrations Guide to the G-Spot
    Cathy Winks $9.50

Herotica 6: A New Collection of Women's Erotica
    ed. Marcy Sheiner $14.95

Herotica 7: New Erotic Fiction by Women
    ed. Marcy Steiner $14.95

Loving Sex: Every Woman's Guide to Sensual Sexuality
    Ellen Nicolas Rathbone $14.95

Exhbitionism for the Shy, revised
    Carol Queen $15.95

Available at your favorite retailer, on-line bookseller or erotic boutique. Many of these titles are also available as ebooks from major ebook retailers.